The Christmas Present

The Pocket Watch Chronicles

By
Ceci Giltenan

This is a work of fiction. The characters, incidents, locations and dialogues in this book are of the author's imagination and are not to be construed as real. Any resemblance to actual events or persons, living or dead, is completely coincidental. Any actual locations mentioned in this book are used fictitiously.

Copyright 2016 by Ceci Giltenan
www.duncurra.com

Cover Design: Earthly Charms

ISBN-10: 1-942623-40-2
ISBN-13: 978-1-942623-40-3
Produced in the USA

Dedication

To my lovely daughter Meghan, who asked if I was a time-traveler—only time will tell my sweet girl. Thank you for always make me laugh. I love you and I look forward to great things to come.

And as ever, my darling Eamon.

Acknowledgements

Thank you to all of my beta-readers: Pat, Anne, K Elizabeth, Virginia, Barb and Ann. I can't tell you how much I value your time and feedback.

A special thank you to my sisters of the heart, Kathryn Lynn Davis and Lily Baldwin. Your support and insight are precious to me.

And finally, thank you to my editor, John Robin. Your eye for detail is remarkable.

Courage is not simply one of the virtues, but the form of every virtue at the testing point.

~ C.S. Lewis

Chapter 1

Tuesday, December 23, 2008
Nona Bay, Florida

Anita Lewis was almost finished baking cookies. She had everyone'd favorites. Her husband, Jim, loved pecan sandies. Katy, their daughter, was fond of peanut butter cookies. Their son, Jack, had been a fan of jam thumbprints, since he was a toddler. His wife adored Anita's toffee bars. And everyone wanted chocolate chip cookies. Anita was taking the last sheet of sugar cookies, her personal favorite, out of the oven mid-morning when the phone rang. The automated voice of the caller id announced, "Katy Lewis."

She grinned, put the cookie sheet on a trivet to cool, turned off the oven and answered the phone. "Hi, Katy, what's up?"

"Hi, Mom."

"Are you all packed and ready? I can't wait to see you tonight."

"Yeah, well, I'm packed, but I have a question for you."

"Shoot."

"On a scale of one to ten, where one is Publix just ran out of eggplant—"

"I hate eggplant."

"I know, Mom. That's the point."

She laughed. "Sorry, go on."

"Okay, so on a scale of one to ten, where one is Publix just ran out of eggplant and ten is North Korea just bombed New York, how upset would you be if I delayed my flight?"

Anita frowned. "Until tomorrow? You know Christmas Eve traffic can be a little crazy. The earlier you get here the better."

"Um…I wouldn't be flying tomorrow either. Probably the evening of Christmas Day but the next day at the latest."

Anita was quiet for a moment. *Nine! On that scale it's a nine.* "I'd rather you fly in tonight. You know, Jack and his family won't be here until Christmas Day." It was the first Christmas since they were born that one of her kids wasn't going to be home on Christmas Eve.

Jack had dropped that bombshell in November. "Mom, you know Erica and I have flown down every Christmas since we were married. The Hales never complain but I know it bothers them."

"Why should it bother them? You live ten minutes away. They can see their daughter and granddaughters practically anytime. They get everyone's birthday, Easter, Thanksgiving, Halloween, every holiday. You can't come down here just any old time."

"I know mom, and we'll come down. It's just, I thought we'd fly on Christmas Day. It's just one day later. That way we can celebrate with both families. Plus, the airfare is a little cheaper on Christmas Day than it is on Christmas Eve. It will also be so much easier not having to haul all the girls' presents from Santa and our presents to each other down there to have on Christmas Day, only to have to bring them and more back up here."

That was certainly true. Anita hadn't been happy about it, but it was only one day later. They would all have Christmas dinner together. It's just that she loved Christmas Eve the most. They had traditions. She had consoled herself with the fact that at least Katy would be there.

Now it looked like she might not even be here until the twenty-sixth.

"Why do you have to postpone your flight, Katy?"

"I don't *have* to, Mom. I'm just considering it."

"But why?"

"It's Tony. We had a really bad argument a few days ago."

By all that was holy, if she was about to say she wanted to spend Christmas with her boyfriend, Anita might burst into tears. "I'm sorry to hear that, but I don't see what that has to do with you catching your flight today."

"Mom, for the last few weeks he's been talking about the future. You know, stuff like buying a house in a nice area with good schools. Like we're planning to get married and have kids."

"But he hasn't asked you to marry him."

"That's just it. He did ask me on Friday night."

Anita wasn't expecting to hear this. It wasn't that she didn't like Tony. No, she had been completely charmed by Tony Soldani the first time she met him, when he and Katy visited in August. Katy had only known him for a couple months but they seemed very well suited for each other.

It wasn't until she and Jim met Katy and Tony at Epcot for a long weekend in October that Anita began to worry. She had asked Katy something about his parents. Katy said she hadn't met them yet. Her comment was very casual, but Anita had seen a flash of hurt in her daughter's eyes. Anita didn't say anything more, but later, when they were alone she'd asked Katy about it.

"Mom, I don't know what to think. Tony is from New Jersey and has the classic, big Italian family, four brothers and a sister, tons of aunts, uncles and cousins. They all seem really close, he talks to his family all the time but he's never invited me to meet them."

"Maybe there hasn't been a good opportunity. You said he's been really busy with work."

"Yeah he has been, but he's gone to see them. He just hasn't asked me. Birthdays are kind of a big deal in their family. His brother Nick's birthday was in August. We'd been dating for nearly two months by then and had made plans to come down here together, but he didn't take me to meet his parents that weekend. Then his brother Luke's birthday was last week and I still wasn't invited. I don't understand it, but I can only think he's not as serious about me as I thought he was."

Anita's heart had broken for Katy. She knew her daughter had fallen hard for Tony and the realization that he didn't feel the same for her had to hurt.

Anita shook her head. She wasn't sure what to say now. If this was confusing to her, it must have Katy wound in knots. "In October you thought things weren't serious, then you came down alone for Thanksgiving."

"I know Mom, but I really liked him and I wanted to keep dating him—at least for a little while longer—but I really didn't think it was going anywhere. That's why I was surprised when he started talking about the future. When he asked me to marry him on Sunday evening, I was stunned. Especially considering the fact that he had driven home Friday night to celebrate his little sister's birthday—and still hadn't asked me to go with him. I'd been so upset about it by the time I saw him on Sunday night, I'd intended to break it off. And he up and asks me to marry him."

"What did you tell him?"

"I said no."

"Oh, Katy."

"He was shocked—I mean completely bowled over. He looked really hurt. He asked me why and I told him I didn't think it was a good idea to marry a man without ever meeting his family. I said I'd given him several opportunities to meet you and dad, and we had to fly to Florida for that. Plus we've gone to dinner at Jack and Erica's lots of times, but he had never once asked me to make the two and a half hour drive to meet his family. I said I figured he was ashamed of me or something and I didn't need that."

"Ouch."

"I know, Mom. He said, 'God, Katy, how could you think that? I love you.' He tried to explain that Italian families are different and he was worried I'd be overwhelmed. He said his family, particularly his mother, can be intimidating at times. He said, 'It's just the way they are, and I love them, but I didn't want them to scare you away.' He hadn't told them about me yet and hadn't wanted to until he was certain I'd marry him."

"That seems, well…"

"I know right? I didn't know what to think and I was too angry to be rational. I told him he'd fouled it up and he might want to reconsider that approach with his next girlfriend."

"Oh, Katy, you didn't."

"I did."

"I'm sorry, sweetheart. But, if you've broken up with him, why aren't you coming home?"

"He came to see me last night. He had two dozen roses and he begged me to hear him out. We talked for hours and I think I understand it now. But the thing is, he wants to take me home now, today. He wants me to meet them and spend Christmas Eve with them. Then he wants to ask me to marry him again. I…Mom, I really love him."

Anita wanted to be angry. She wanted to say, *Tony knew you were planning to come down here, he can wait until you're back,* but she couldn't. She remembered what it was like to be young and in love and then to fight. All couples fight. The work of marriage was loving each other through a fight and resolving the issue. And the faster a problem was addressed, the easier it was to heal. "I know you love him, Katy. And I think he is a good man—even if it would have been better to address the issue of his family earlier."

"He was afraid of losing me."

"And that's a healthy fear. He needs to value and adore you."

"So—Publix is out of eggplant?"

Anita laughed. "More like Publix is out of my favorite flavor of ice cream but they'll have it again in a few days."

"Thanks, Mom. I love you."

"I love you too, Katy."

"I'll call you tomorrow evening."

"Great. I'll talk to you then."

Anita hung up the phone. She stood looking around. Everything was ready. The trees were decorated, presents wrapped, cookies baked. She'd even managed to get the Christmas cards in the mail this morning. They wouldn't arrive by Christmas, but it would have to do. Some years she was so late, she didn't send them at all. For one of the first times in living memory, she was completely ready for Christmas. The only thing missing was her family. Her nest was empty.

She burst into tears. She understood. She really did. It didn't stop her from feeling sorry for herself and giving into that self-pity for a few minutes.

She had barely managed to regain control when her husband called. "Hi, Jim."

"Hi hon. Anything new there today? Any calls?"

That was all it took. She started crying again. "Katy called."

"What's wrong, did something happen?"

"She's fine." Anita pulled herself together to explain what had happened.

When she had finished, Jim said, "I guess I understand his reasons."

"You think so?"

"Yeah. If there had been anyone or anything in my life that I'd thought might have pushed you away, I damn well would have avoided it until I was absolutely certain you were mine."

"Really?" Those words surprised her. But the idea that Jim had ever been unsure of himself and her love for him was sweet and touching.

"Really."

"Christmas Eve won't be the same without the kids here." Her voice wavered, on the edge of tears again.

"Christmas might not ever be the same."

"Anita, you're upset over nothing. They're growing older. We're growing older. It was bound to happen. They'll all be here in a few days."

She loved him, but he was such a man sometimes. She wasn't upset over nothing but there was no point arguing.

"Listen, I called because I'm going to be late this evening. Today has been one massive cluster-fuck. If we don't get it sorted this evening, we'll all be working late tomorrow too."

"Should I plan dinner for later? Seven?"

"Don't plan on me for dinner."

She sighed, disappointed. She didn't want to spend this evening alone, thinking about how alone she was. "Fine. I'll probably go to the mall and pick up a few last minute things. Maybe I'll just get something there to eat."

"That sounds like a plan. I'll see you later. Love you."

"Love you too. Bye."

Chapter 2

Later that day
Sandy Cove Mall
Nona Bay, Florida

Anita Lewis sat at a table in the food court, staring morosely at her empty ice cream dish. *I shouldn't have eaten that. It didn't make me feel better.* She sighed. "Now instead of just depressed, I feel fat…and depressed. Well done Anita."

"What's that dear?"

Anita looked up. A sharply dressed elderly woman stood near her table with a disposable cup of some warm beverage in her hand. Anita hadn't noticed the woman before. "I'm sorry? Did you ask me something?"

The elderly woman smiled. "My name's Gertrude. Do you mind if I sit down with ye to drink my tea? It's rather crowded here today."

"Please do."

Gertrude spoke with a rich Scottish burr that Anita could have listened to all day.

When the woman had settled herself, she smiled at Anita. "Now, as I was walking past, I thought ye said something to me and I didn't quite hear it."

Anita shook her head. "No, I was just talking to myself. It's not important."

Gertrude canted her head to one side, as if sizing Anita up. "Now, ye see, I think it might have been important. Things one speaks aloud normally are, whether we realize it or not."

"Trust me, it was completely insignificant. I'm simply regretting the ice cream I just ate."

"And why is that? Did ye not enjoy it? Was it not good?"

Anita laughed. "No it was very good. It's my favorite in fact. Technically it was frozen custard and I absolutely love frozen custard. Clive's makes the best in the area. In fact, it's some of the best I've ever eaten."

"Then why on earth would ye regret enjoying a cup of it?"

Anita glanced down at herself. Wasn't it obvious? The last thing she needed was a few more calories. She was fifty-eight years old and her elastic waist white capris had bypassed "mom pants", landing squarely in the realm of "grandma pants". She had intended for the slightly over-large Christmas tee-shirt to camouflage her round belly and chubby thighs but she knew it wasn't fooling anyone. Still, on top of everything else that had happened, she wasn't going to tell this elegant stranger about her love-hate relationship with food. "It's hard to explain."

The woman narrowed her eyes. "Perhaps I can explain it. Something is bothering ye. Ye came to the mall to do some last-minute shopping, hoping that the Christmas music and decorations would cheer you up, but it didn't work. Ye are, in fact, feeling even worse now. And on top of that, ye have spent the last hour 'should-ing' all over yerself."

"Excuse me? What did you say?"

"Ye heard me correctly. I said ye've been 'should-ing' on yerself. *Should-ing.* 'I *should* be happy, everyone else is;' 'I *should* have more Christmas spirit;' I *should* have sent my cards out earlier;' 'I *should* have bypassed the frozen custard;' 'I *should* be a better'—well any number of things, wife, mother, daughter, friend, fill in the blank for yerself."

Anita blinked. Tears welled in her eyes. She couldn't speak.

Gertrude leaned forward, taking Anita's hands in hers. Her touch was warm and comforting.

"Those tears tell me I'm right and they're telling ye how harmful it is to 'should' on oneself."

"But it's all true."

"No it is not." Gertrude's voice was stern, almost angry. "Ye've been happily married to yer husband for thirty-two years. Ye've weathered storms together and come out stronger. Ye have two children who are a credit to ye both. Ye've raised them well and they enrich this world because of it. Worrying about the timing of yer Christmas cards is beyond unimportant. Yer true friends will enjoy hearing from ye whether the card arrives before Christmas or in February, and they are the only ones who matter. Ye love frozen custard and ye don't have it very often. Why on earth would ye dim the pleasure of enjoying a treat ye adore by piling guilt on top of it? Ye're a beautiful woman, just as ye are. Why do ye tell yerself otherwise?"

A lump rose in Anita's throat and she wouldn't meet Gertrude's eyes.

The old woman continued. "I'll tell ye why. Because something has made ye sad and like so many people, when ye're sad, all of yer fears and doubts surface, making ye feel worse. So tell me what's weighing so heavily on yer heart, Anita?"

"It's silly…wait, how did you know my name? I didn't tell you that. And how did you know those other things, about my husband and children?"

Gertrude smiled. "It's a gift. I know everything I need to know about ye, when I need to know it."

Anita wasn't sure why she believed the old woman, but warmth flowed from her and Anita was suddenly confident that this was true. Still, she couldn't help asking, "If you know so much about me, then why don't you know what's bothering me?"

Gertrude smiled indulgently. "I do know what's bothering ye. But I'm not sure ye do—or at least ye haven't fully admitted it to yerself yet. So tell me. Name it. Put it into words."

Anita's chin trembled. "Nothing is going right and Christmas is ruined."

Instead of arguing with her, Gertrude smiled. "There, ye've said it. Christmas is ruined. And, truth told, ye feel guilty for feeling that, much less saying it."

Anita nodded, not trusting herself to speak.

"So, now that ye've put it out there, tell me why Christmas is ruined."

Anita sighed and launched into the tale.

When she had finished, Gertrude smiled at her. "So, there ye go, *should-ing* on yerself again."

"I didn't say—"

"I know ye didn't say it, but ye thought it. Ye thought, 'My children are adults and both of them have made practical, loving choices that result in their not being here for Christmas Eve. I *should* not be angry or disappointed over that, but I am.'"

Anita smiled weakly. "Well it's true. You said it, I raised good kids. I have no right to be disappointed when they prove it."

"Ye're wrong. Ye have the right to feel whatever ye feel. Ye supported both of them in their decisions didn't ye?"

"Yes."

"Excellent. That doesn't mean ye can't feel disappointment too."

"But, I fear Christmas is never going to be the same again."

"Oh, my darling girl, change is not always bad. Things evolve. Most babes leave the warmth and quiet of their mother's womb kicking and screaming. The outside world is foreign and cold. Their lives change in an instant and they don't like it. However, after they've experienced life, I doubt there are many people who would choose to go back to the womb."

Anita sighed. "I see yer point. I just wish things were different. I wish the world wasn't so big. I wish my children could have found jobs closer to home."

Gertrude cocked her head. "Some would say technology is such that the world grows smaller and smaller."

"It doesn't feel small to me. There was a time when kids settled in the same town, sometimes the same house they grew up in. Life revolved around a huge extended family. It sounds like Katy's boyfriend's family is still like that."

"We often want what we can't have and fail to see the gifts we've been given."

"If being alone on Christmas Eve is a gift, where do I return it?"

Gertrude laughed. "Would ye return a clothing gift without trying it on?"

Anita wasn't ready to look for silver linings. "I might."

Gertrude laughed again. "Maybe I can help you fix Christmas."

"That's kind of you, but you can't. I mean, even if you had the power to bring my children here by tomorrow evening, I've already told you, I understand and support their choices. I'm just disappointed. I wouldn't want to change their minds or plans."

"It's not *their* minds or plans I intend to change."

Anita smiled. "You can try, but I don't think anything will make this better. It is just something to be endured."

"I see. Well, Anita, sometimes perspective is everything. Close yer eyes."

"What?"

"Go ahead, close yer eyes. I want to show ye something."

Anita shrugged and closed her eyes. She listened as Gertrude rummaged in her bag.

"Ah, here it is. Now open yer eyes."

Gertrude held a silver Christmas tree ball, encircled by a red ribbon tied in a bow at the top of the ball. "What is this?"

"A Christmas tree ornament."

"What color is it?"

"Silver."

"I believe it's gold."

"I'm sorry Gertrude, it's clearly silver."

"Ye're absolutely certain?"

"Yes, it's silver with a red ribbon."

Gertrude turned the sphere ninety degrees. "It is only silver from yer perspective." The other half was, indeed, gold. She smiled. "When one changes one's perspective—looks at something from a different angle—they may see it differently. Ye came to the mall today, hoping to see things that would make ye happy. But instead, it has only intensified the sadness ye were feeling. Perhaps that's because ye can't see another perspective."

"I'm not sure that there is another perspective."

Gertrude smiled indulgently. "Of course there is. There's always another perspective. Do ye see the girl working the register at Clive's?"

Anita nodded.

"She has to work until closing tomorrow."

"Poor girl."

"That is only from yer perspective. She is happy to work tomorrow. This is her first job. It is the first time she's earned her own money. It's only minimum wage, and she's a student so she can't work many hours. Nevertheless, the money she earns is hers. She has spent this season shopping for and buying a little present for everyone in her family with her very own money. She's never been able to do that, and she is very proud and excited about it. Aye, she has to work Christmas Eve but she is thankful for her job and the modest income it brings her. She considers it a small sacrifice."

"That's lovely." Anita wasn't sure how Gertrude knew this. Perhaps she knew the girl or had chatted with her. Gertrude seemed to be the chatty sort.

"Aye. Perspective. Now, do ye see the three women at the table behind me? An older woman and her two daughters chatting away merrily?"

"Yes." Anita had a hard time keeping the wistful tone from her voice.

"This is the first time in fifteen years that both of her daughters have come down here at the same time to celebrate Christmas with her."

Anita's brow drew together.

Gertrude nodded. "One comes one year and the other the next. All these years, this was their way to make certain their parents always had a few family members visit over the holidays. They also reasoned having everyone in at once would make the house too crowded and create too much work for their mom. From their perspective this was the perfect solution. Their mom literally had to beg in order to convince both of them to bring their families at the same time."

"I guess I understand their reasoning, but still, it's a shame." Anita wondered how Gertrude could know this. They must be friends.

"Aye, it is. But what their mother hasn't told them is that she's been diagnosed with an aggressive cancer."

Anita's hand flew to her mouth. "The poor woman."

"She believes, and she's right, that this is her last Christmas here. She didn't tell them that. She doesn't want to *ruin* their Christmas with the weight of this news. But she also doesn't want next year to roll around and have one of them feel guilty that they missed the opportunity for one last Christmas with mom."

Anita was speechless.

Gertrude smiled. "Again, perspective. She isn't worrying about what's to come, or gnashing her teeth about the unfairness of cancer. She decided to give her girls and their families a priceless present—memories of a happy Christmas. She vowed to simply savor every possible minute and is enjoying perhaps the most wonderful Christmas season of her life."

Anita looked at the woman again. Indeed her face was wreathed in smiles and she seemed blissfully happy. "Perspective certainly does change perception."

"Aye, it does."

Anita smiled. "You were right, changing my perspective helps. It doesn't make it a lot easier, but it helps. Thank you for reminding me of that."

Gertrude waved a hand. "'Twas my pleasure." She took a sip of her tea. "So, Anita, what would ye do if ye knew for certain this were yer last Christmas on Earth? Acknowledging that nothing can change the plans set into motion, that is."

Anita frowned. "Is it?"

"I doubt it, but I don't know for certain. As I told ye, I know what I need to know, when I need to know it."

"I guess if I knew for certain this was my last Christmas ever, I would do what the lady at the next table is doing. I would try to spend as much time as possible with my family and make it memorable."

"I'm certain ye would." Gertrude canted her head to one side, appearing to consider her for a moment. "Now, my dear, as ye were telling me about yer children not being able to be with ye on Christmas Eve, ye left something unsaid."

Anita's brow furrowed. "No, I didn't. I told you everything."

"Ye told me the facts, but ye didn't tell me everything. There is a little fear, deep in yer heart, that ye wouldn't give voice to."

This woman was extraordinary. Anita could only stare at her for a moment, and try to blink back tears.

Gertrude said nothing, apparently willing to wait as long as she needed to.

Finally Anita sighed. "I'm afraid—" She swallowed hard. "I'm afraid last Christmas Eve was the last one I will ever spend with both children and I didn't realize it at the time."

Gertrude smiled as a teacher would at an excellent student. "Precisely. And ye've just said, if ye knew this were yer last Christmas with them, ye'd make it as memorable as possible. What would ye do, if ye had the opportunity to give someone else one last memorable Christmas with their family? If ye could do that, would ye?"

Anita smiled. "I doubt that will ever happen. I lack your peculiar skill. But, yes, I would if I could."

A very serious expression crossed Gertrude's face. "I knew ye were the right person for this task."

"I don't understand."

"I need for ye to do something but I must explain a few things first. Will ye spare me a few moments and listen?"

"Of course."

"Anita, ye accepted that I know a great many things about ye, although we've never met before."

"Yes. I'm not sure why…"

"The 'why' is simple. I am infinitely trustworthy. I was made so by the Creator and I would not—cannot—break that trust. Even as I'm telling ye this, ye know it's true."

Anita nodded, a little amazed. She *didn't* have a single doubt.

"There is a family I know of, the Carrs, a wonderful, large, loving family. Agnes, the matriarch of that family, is about to become very ill. In fact, over the last few months her health has deteriorated and her family fears she isn't long for this world. Their deepest desire is to have one last Christmas season with her. But, as things stand at the moment, she will have a stroke tomorrow which will ultimately claim her life."

"I'm so sorry."

Gertrude smiled. "Death isn't always something to be sorry for. Agnes is ready."

"But it is never easy to lose a loved one. When it happens at a holiday it somehow makes things feel worse."

"Aye, it does. And I would like to give her family one more wonderful Christmas with her. But doing so means she would have to linger in a frail, failing body. Something she fears beyond death itself."

"I don't understand what I can do to help."

"I know ye don't understand yet, but if there was a way that ye could give her family another Christmas with her while saving her from a fate she dreads, and still spend Christmas with yer own family, would ye consider doing it?"

"Of course I would."

"Well then, I assure ye it is possible. Given ye've accepted I have unusual abilities, please keep an open mind as I tell ye this next bit."

"I will."

"Excellent." She opened her handbag and pulled out a gold pocket watch. "This pocket watch is a conduit for time travel. It allows two souls in different times to trade places."

"You're joking."

Gertrude arched a brow at her. "Open mind, Anita."

"Okay, I'm sorry. How does it work?"

"Basically, a person who accepts the pocket watch takes it home, tells it a return word, and puts it around their neck or in a pocket before they go to sleep. When they wake up, their soul and consciousness will be in someone else's body in another time."

"That's it?"

Gertrude chuckled. "Well there is a bit more to it but the rules are fairly simple." She opened the watch, showing it to Anita. "It only has one hand. This hand will advance one day for every day the time traveler is away but only one second will pass in the present. A person using the watch has up to sixty days to experience another life in another time."

"So if I did this I would be in some other time for two months, but when I returned it would be one minute after I left?"

"That's essentially right. So ye'd be able to help the Carrs, and still be here for Christmas. But, ye don't have to stay the entire time. In fact, ye must choose to say yer return word sometime within the sixty days, or ye won't be able to return home ever. And when ye do say it, yer soul will return to yer own body instantly."

Anita could scarcely believe what she was hearing. But deep in her soul she knew Gertrude was telling her the truth. "Okay, let's just say I believe this works. What happens when I return? Agnes will be back in her failing body and also have lost up to sixty days. I think that would be terrible."

Gertrude nodded. "And it would be if that happened, but it won't. Setting Agnes's specific case aside, normally the person into whose body the time traveler goes will have done something to set events in motion that will result in their death and the time traveler does something immediately that prevents it. Therefore, as the other person's life was over, when the time traveler returns to their own time, the other person's body dies and their soul moves on. If, by chance, the time traveler chooses not to return, their body dies here and the other soul moves on."

"But this time is different?"

"It is very different. As I said before, in this case, Agnes will have a stroke on Christmas Eve. If nothing changes, she will die at that moment. If ye accept the watch and enter her body, ye'll have the strength and will to live on for a while even in a very frail, weak body."

"You're sure this will help? Even if I keep her alive until after Christmas what good will it do? I might be in Agnes's body, but I'm not really her. I'm a stranger. I won't know anything about her family, which I'm sure would be distressing to everyone. And in the end Agnes will die the moment I choose to come back."

"All valid concerns. But first, let me ask ye something. Do ye remember the last Christmas before yer grandfather died?"

Anita smiled and nodded. "I was just a little girl. He had lung cancer and was on oxygen. He couldn't talk much, but he was there, smiling, watching as we unwrapped presents and played games."

"So it was simply the warmth of his presence which made that Christmas special?"

"Yes, I suppose it was."

"It will be the same in this case. Her great-grandchildren will forever hold dear the memories of cuddling on her lap, telling her stories and singing songs to her. That is a truly precious gift to give them. But as I've said before, this time everything is a little different. While it is true you'll have your own mind and soul, you will be in her body with her brain and in this case, she will be aware of her family's love, just not her failing body."

"But how do I explain not knowing anything?"

Gertrude smiled. "You won't have to explain. Remember, Agnes will have just had a stroke. She'll be very weak and unable to speak well. Time travelers are generally able to understand and speak the language of their host and ye'll be able to understand what is said to ye—it'll feel no different than English does. But ye'll not be able to speak her language, at least not much because, as a result of the stroke, she won't be able to."

"Will she—that is to say, *I*—be in pain?"

"Aye. She is elderly and has the aches and pains that come with her age. And she will be left seriously weakened by the stroke."

"And I'll feel all of that?"

Gertrude nodded solemnly. "Aye. Every gift has its price and this one will not be easy to pay. But I promise, ye'll never regret it."

Anita's head was spinning. She was being offered a chance to give an invaluable gift to this family and although it wouldn't be easy, in the long run it would literally take less than a minute of her time. Finally, her resolve set, she nodded. "I'll do it."

Gertrude smiled and a warmth and peace, unlike any she had ever known, washed over Anita. "I knew I could count on ye. Now ye've accepted, I can tell ye a bit more. As I said, ye'll enter the body of a very dear old soul by the name of Agnes. Lady Agnes Carr, that is."

"Lady? A noblewoman?"

"Aye. She lived in the Scottish Highlands a very long time ago—in the thirteenth century—and she is the grandmother of Logan Carr, Laird of Clan Carr."

Anita was stunned. "The thirteenth century? Medieval Scotland? I had no idea you meant—good heavens that's…that's…"

Gertrude nodded. "Over seven hundred years ago. Aye. Lady Agnes has lived a long and full life. She is greatly loved by her family and clan and as I've already said, nothing will actually keep her from dying. Her time on Earth is done. Indeed, Lady Agnes herself is ready to go home to the Creator. She is eighty-two years old and—"

"Eighty-two? In the thirteenth century? I thought the average life expectancy was forty or so."

"That's true. However, that number includes the exceedingly high death rate among infants and children, which brings the average down. People who lived to adulthood, especially those in the upper classes who didn't experience as much hardship, generally lived longer. That said, ye are right, eighty-two is quite an advanced age to reach for someone living in that era and it is the exception rather than the rule. But as I've said, Lady Agnes is eight-two years old. She is tired and in pain. If yer soul enters her body, she will not die on Christmas Eve. Her family and clan will not be thrown into mourning and forever remember that their beloved matriarch died on Christmas Eve. While they will be fully aware that it is their last one, they will have one more Christmas season with her. At the same time, Agnes herself will rest peacefully in yer body, feeling her family's abundant love and be spared suffering from the stroke which inevitably will end her life."

"Suffering. That's the part that scares me."

"I can understand that. But in addition to knowing ye've given this great woman and her family an amazing gift, ye'll also experience Christmas as a thirteenth century noblewoman, amid a large and loving clan. Ye've always been fond of history."

She had been. She'd taught sixth grade for years but her favorite subject was history. This was an incredible opportunity to see it firsthand. But the rest was daunting. Even in today's world, with all its technology, dealing with the sequelae of a profound stroke is hard. And the *aches and pains that come with her age* were nothing to look forward to either. At fifty-eight, Anita had days when her joints were stiff and ached, but she could just go to the medicine cabinet and take an analgesic. She couldn't imagine what it must be like for Agnes. She was on the verge of backing out, when she remembered how she'd felt after Katy's call. Mixed in with everything was fear and regret. The fear that Christmas Eve would never be the same and the regret that she hadn't savored it more last year. Could she do this? Give this gift to another family and a venerable old woman?

"Can ye do it?" asked Gertrude, echoing Anita's thoughts.

Anita nodded. "Yes. I can." After all, it was only a couple of days.

Gertrude beamed. "I knew ye would. Now there are a few other details ye need to know. As I said, because of the

stroke, ye'll not be able to speak Gaelic clearly. Ye'll be able
to communicate a little, but yer words will be slurred. It will
be difficult."

"But if I can't speak clearly, how will I say the return
word when the time comes?"

"The stroke will only have affected Agnes's ability to
speak Gaelic because of the damage to that part of her brain.
Because the stroke will not have affected yer mind, ye will be
able to speak English without difficulty and yer return word
will be in English."

"Okay." Anita gave a sigh of relief.

"So, back to business," Gertrude said as she handed
Anita the pocket watch. "I must be sure ye know exactly
what to do."

"Tonight when I go to bed, I tell the watch a return
word, put it around my neck and go to sleep. I will wake in
Agnes's body. The watch will advance one second for every
day I am in the past. I must put the watch around my neck
and say the return word within sixty days to return to the
present. My goal is to stay through Christmas."

"That sums it up, except you don't have to have it
around yer neck to say the word. As long as it is in the same
time as you are, it will work from wherever it is. That's one
of the miracles of the pocket watch."

"That's good to know."

"Now, regarding yer return word, it must be
something ye won't say accidentally." Gertrude looked at her
for a moment. Her eyes stopped on Anita's Christmas tee-
shirt and she smiled.

Anita glanced down at it and smiled too. It was from
Beall's, her favorite department store, and, worked in
rhinestones on it, was a flamingo wearing a Santa hat. "We
do things a little differently here in subtropical Florida."

Gertrude grinned. "I like it. And it gives me an idea
for yer word. Might I suggest 'flamingo'?"

"That's perfect. I love flamingos."

Gertrude winked. "I thought ye might." She stood up. "Now, it's been a pleasure but I must be on my way and ye need to finish yer shopping."

As Gertrude started to walk away, Anita called, "Wait. How do I get the watch back to you?"

Gertrude waved a hand. "Ye needn't worry about it. The watch will find me when ye return."

As Gertrude walked away, a group of teenage girls, laden with bags and chattering happily, walked by. When they had passed, Anita couldn't see Gertrude anywhere.

Anita laughed. "I guess that shouldn't surprise me."

Chapter 3

Later that evening

Jim wasn't home that evening until after eight and he fell asleep watching the ten o'clock news. Anita had trouble waking him, but eventually she got him up and into bed. By the time she had washed her face and brushed her teeth, he was sound asleep and snoring.

Before getting into bed, she retrieved the pocket watch from her purse. When she'd been with Gertrude, everything seemed logical and made sense. Now, with the strength of Gertrude's presence gone, it all seemed ridiculous. She very nearly put the watch back into her purse, until a little voice inside her said, *But what if…*

Anita's resolve strengthened. It might not work, but if it didn't, the worst thing that would happen was she'd wake in the morning with the watch around her neck feeling a little silly.

"Okay, here we go." She opened the pocket watch, but just as she said, "My return word is 'flamingo'," Jim rolled over, giving a snore that was so loud it nearly rattled the windows. Nothing happened. She frowned. Better to be safe. "Just in case you didn't hear me, my return word is *flamingo*." She wasn't sure what she expected, but still nothing happened. She shrugged, closed the pocket watch, put the chain around her neck and curled up in bed.

She laid there for a while, wide awake. She glanced at the clock on the nightstand—it was ten forty-five.

She rolled over, trying to get comfortable, but still couldn't manage to sleep. She glanced at the clock again—eleven o'clock.

Truthfully, this wasn't unusual. Normally it took her at least forty-five minutes to fall asleep and that was when she read for a while first.

At eleven fifteen, she opened a book and flicked on the tiny reading light. Even so, it was after midnight before she felt relaxed enough to sleep and put the book away.

~ * ~

It felt as if she'd only been asleep for a moment when her eyes popped open. She was sitting at a wooden table in what appeared to be the great hall of…*a castle*. She wanted to look around, but the pain in her head was blinding. She felt herself slump forward. *This is it. Agnes is having the stroke.*

"Grandmother? Grandmother, what's the matter?" said a sweet feminine voice.

"Good heavens! Agnes, is something wrong?" the voice belonged to an older woman.

Anita tried to raise her head but couldn't. She tried to put her hands on the table and push herself up. Only the right hand did her bidding and she managed to raise up a little.

By this time the younger woman was at her side, cradling Anita's head in her small hands. "Grandmother? Oh, no. *Grandmother.*" She wrapped her arms around Anita. "Mother, we need to get her to her bed. I fear she's had a stroke of apoplexy." She looked across the room. "Broc, send someone for Logan and I need someone to carry Lady Agnes upstairs."

A boy who looked to be about nine or ten years old appeared at her left side. "Mama, is there anything I can do?"

He looked frightened and Anita wanted to reach out to him, comfort him, but her left arm hung useless at her side.

Almost instantly, several other children appeared behind him. "Mama, what's wrong with Great Granny?" asked a little girl who appeared to be six or seven.

"Granny is ill. Evan, we aren't going to have lessons today. I need ye to take Malina and the twins to the nursery and tell Nanny Peggy what's happened. She'll mind all of ye till I've taken care of Granny."

There was a flurry of activity as the young woman called more orders. Before Anita knew what was happening, a strong young man lifted her in his arms and carried her up a winding stone staircase. He took her into a room containing an ornately carved bed, which stood under a canopy hanging from the ceiling, and laid her gently in the bed.

Both women who'd been with her downstairs were right behind him.

The pain Anita felt in her head was excruciating. The bright morning sun flooding the room only made it worse. She closed her eyes.

She must have lost consciousness because when next she opened her eyes, slanting shadows suggested that it was late afternoon.

"Grandmother, ye've joined us again." The young woman from earlier sat beside her, holding her right hand.

Anita tried to answer, *I was asleep*, but all that came out was "Ahhhhwaaaeep." She frowned and tried again. "Ahhhh waaaaas ssssleeeep."

"Ye were asleep?"

Anita squeezed her hand.

"Yes, ye were." The voice came from a handsome man standing near the hearth, who appeared to be in his late thirties.

The young woman caressed Anita's cheek. "Grandmother, I think ye've suffered an apoplexy. That's why it's hard to talk and ye have no strength on yer left side."

Even though Anita had known this would happen, it was still very frightening to be in a body that didn't follow her commands and among people she didn't know and with whom she couldn't communicate easily.

She pushed at the bed with her right elbow. She was uncomfortable and wanted to readjust her position, but got nowhere. She also realized her bladder was full and aching.

She needed help. *I need to get up* became:
"Ahhheeeeeuhhhhhhhhp."

"I'm sorry, Grandmother, I can't understand you."

A tear slipped down Anita's cheek. Maybe she'd been out of it for days. Maybe Christmas was over and she could say the word. She needed to find out. She drew on everything in her. "Whaaaaaaa daaaay?"

"What day is it? It's Christmas Eve," answered the man.

Damn. She had to stay. And she had to pee. She tried again. "Uhhhp. Peeeeee."

"She needs to use the chamber pot," said the older woman who had been in the great hall. Anita hadn't noticed her sitting on the other side of the bed until that moment. "Logan, bring it to the side of the bed and we'll help her up."

The younger woman was already trying to help her into a sitting position. But before they could get her up, she felt warm moisture spread out beneath her. She'd wet herself. Embarrassed, she couldn't keep the tears at bay.

The young woman stroked Anita's hair. "It's all right, Grandmother. We'll take care of it. Let's get you onto the chamber pot just in case you still need it. Logan, go and fetch some serving women to help change the linens. Your mother and I can handle this."

With the girl on one side and the older woman on the other, they managed to help Anita stand on her right leg. They lifted her skirts and helped her pivot onto the chamber pot.

"Maggie, it's probably best to get her wet clothes off while she's up. I'll find a night-rail to put on her." The older woman opened a chest and after a moment's searching pulled out a long, white nightgown that looked like it might have been made from wool.

Maggie began unlacing the clothing Anita wore. She pulled off the outer dress then untied ribbons at Anita's neck that held on a voluminous white garment. It wasn't until then that Anita realized the watch was around her neck.

A moment later, Maggie gasped as she pulled the white undergarment over Anita's head.

Anita searched her brain frantically. Had watches been invented yet? How would she explain this? The fact was, she couldn't explain it. She was physically unable to.

Maggie lifted the watch from around her neck and turned it over in her hands before opening it. Then she captured Anita's gaze. "You're a time traveler."

Anita gaped at her. "You know?" Anita felt as shocked as Maggie looked. The words came out clear and smooth—in English.

"And you speak English." Maggie's voice changed and Anita knew she'd spoken to her in English as well.

The older woman on the other side of the room stood wide-eyed, watching them. "What is it?"

Maggie held up the watch for her to see. "She's a time traveler." This time the words must have been Gaelic.

The other woman's eyes went wide. "Hide that before the other women get here."

Maggie nodded, slipping it around her own neck, under her clothes. "I'm sure this is all overwhelming. My name is Maggie Carr and I used the watch years ago but the only people who know are my mother by marriage, Lady Davina Carr," Maggie gestured to the other woman, "and my husband, Logan, who is the laird of this clan. Ye're Lady Agnes Carr, Logan's grandmother and Davina's mother by marriage. We'll just get you sorted here and after the serving women leave we can talk freely."

Anita knew Maggie had spoken in Gaelic, just by the tone of her voice—and clearly she'd done it so Lady Davina would understand.

Maggie worked quickly to clean Anita up and dress her. Serving women arrived, removed the soiled bedding and remade the bed.

One of the serving women addressed Maggie. "My lady, I'd be happy to sit with Lady Agnes if ye'd like a wee break."

Maggie smiled. "Thank ye, Freya. Later perhaps."

When Anita was alone again with the two women, Maggie sat beside her, taking her hand again. "Gertrude gave me the watch eleven years ago. I fell in love with Logan and stayed."

"Good heavens, child, what did ye just say?"

Maggie turned to her mother-in-law. "I spoke English to her and told her how long I've been here." Turning back to Anita she said in Gaelic, "I was a nurse in my own time. I expect ye can still speak English but are having trouble with Gaelic because of the damage to Agnes's brain caused by the stroke. If ye're able to understand me, I'll speak in Gaelic so Davina can understand."

Anita nodded.

"What's yer name?"

"Anita. Anita Lewis."

"It's nice to meet ye, Anita. Now, ye'll have to help me a bit. I know exactly how the pocket watch works, but I don't understand what's happened here. Agnes could not have done anything to bring on the stroke and as far as I know, ye could do nothing to prevent her from dying with it."

"According to Gertrude, this time it's a little different. It's true neither Agnes nor I did anything to affect the stroke. It was inevitable. It's a long story, but the bottom line is that Gertrude knew you were all hoping for one more Christmas with Agnes, while Agnes herself wanted to pass quickly, without having this happen." Anita motioned to her left side.

Maggie repeated what Anita had said, for Davina. Then, turning back to Anita asked, "You accepted the watch knowing this would happen?"

"Yes. Like I said, it's a long story. But it was meant to be a gift to both Agnes and her family. As I understand it from Gertrude, Agnes will feel your love, but not the ravages of the stroke and the family will have the memories of one last Christmas. Although, now that you know I'm not Agnes, I'm not sure that's true anymore."

"Well, we're the only two who know." Maggie motioned to herself and Davina. "And we also know that, thanks to ye, Agnes will pass painlessly, as she would have wished to. Ye've done a wonderful thing for us." A tear slipped down Maggie's cheek. "I will miss her dreadfully, but I'm confident I'll see her again."

"And there's another thing," added Davina. "If Maggie and I didn't know, we would push for ye to stay abed and rest, hoping for some recovery. But now, knowing what we do about yer purpose, we'll make every effort to keep ye up and surrounded by loved ones."

Anita smiled, or she tried to. She could feel only one side of her mouth turn up. "Then ye believe there is purpose in all of this."

Maggie chuckled. "There usually is where Gertrude is concerned."

"I'd love to hear your story."

"I will tell it to ye before ye go. However, if we are going to get ye downstairs, among the clan and family, and get ye to Mass tonight, we have to make some plans."

"Will we tell Logan?" asked Lady Davina.

Maggie furrowed her brow. "I'm not sure. Let's not immediately. If something arises that will make it necessary, we'll tell him then."

"There was a soft knock at the door."

"Come in," called Davina.

A little brown head poked in. It was the boy Anita had seen in the great hall.

"Evan, son, come in," said Maggie.

"Is Great Granny all right?"

Maggie nodded. "She is for now. She has had what we call an apoplexy. It is something that happens inside one's head. It has left her very weak. In fact, she can't move anything on her left side well at all. It has also made it very hard for her to talk. But she hears and understands perfectly well."

Anita reached her right hand towards the little boy.

He came close to the bed and slipped his small hand into her old gnarled one. "Can I stay with ye for a while, Great Granny?"

Anita smiled as best she could and nodded.

"Evan, Granny and I have some things to take care of. I'll send Freya up with Malina, then perhaps the three of ye can keep Great Granny company?"

He nodded vigorously.

Anita spent the rest of the afternoon being entertained by Agnes's two oldest great-grandchildren. And just as Gertrude had said, the experience reminded her poignantly of the last Christmas with her own grandfather. They talked and played and she just soaked it in. After several hours she felt herself begin to doze and Freya stepped in. "Now, Evan, Malina, run find yer mama and tell her I'll stay with yer great granny while she takes a wee rest."

Chapter 4

Maggie and Davina spent the rest of the afternoon, overseeing the creation of a comfortable litter. It had short legs on it to hold it about a foot and a half off the ground. They had it fitted with a small, wool-filled mattress and pillows so that Anita could be propped into a sitting position.

"What is all this for?" asked Logan when he saw the finished product.

"It's so Agnes can be easily carried to Mass and attend the upcoming feasts."

Logan frowned. "Maggie, I'm surprised at ye. She's just suffered and apoplexy, she needs rest."

Maggie looked at Logan for a moment, trying to decide what to tell him. The truth was usually the best option, but in this case she could be truthful without giving all the details. "Logan, do ye agree that sometimes certain needs outweigh others?"

"Certainly, but given her condition, I wouldn't think getting her to Mass was overly important."

She took his hands in hers. "My love, the apoplexy was very bad. And yer grandmother has been declining over the last few months to the point that she was already frail."

"All the more reason to insist she rest."

Maggie shook her head. "The truth is, no amount of rest is going to make the quality of her life better. No matter what I do, she will not live long. This is most surely her last Christmas and our last Christmas with her."

"But—"

"No Logan. Yer grandmother is one of the most vital, energetic people I've ever known and she was already in her seventies when I met her. Even if staying in bed and being tended would keep her with us another year—which it will not—it would be at the expense of her comfort, happiness and dignity. And, without the ability to treat the stroke or the underlying conditions which may have caused it, it is only a matter of time before she has another one. She will not be with us long. I know this and so does she. She wants to celebrate Christmas as best she can. I will not deny her that."

Logan looked away for a moment. "Ye're certain?"

"Absolutely. Let's make a few last wonderful memories with her. Maretta is too young but the other children aren't. Let's not have them remember her sick and in bed. That is not who she is and it's the last thing she'd want."

Logan nodded. The sadness in his eyes tore at Maggie's heart and tears filled her eyes. Letting go of his hands, she wrapped her arms around him. "I couldn't love her more if she were my own grandmother. If there was anything at all I could do to change this, ye know I would. This is what she wants."

~ * ~

Anita dozed off and on into the evening. Each time she woke feeling the pain in Agnes's body and being unable to move easily, she experienced a moment of panic. But one glance around the room reminded her of the decision she'd made to accept the watch. Although she thought she'd known what to expect, she could never have imagined the reality of it. Even without the miracles of modern medicine, the normal discomfort of an elderly body might have been tolerable if she'd had full mobility. She had never fully appreciated how much simply being able to move easily and slightly readjust her position helped lessen one pain or another. With effort she could move her left arm some, but her left leg was useless. If she wanted to turn on her side, or bend her left knee, or even just move her foot slightly, she needed someone to help her. The fact that she couldn't communicate exactly what she needed unless she was alone with Maggie made things infinitely worse. Anita's solace in all of this was that it was Christmas Eve and she wouldn't have to endure it long. She could say the word in a couple of days.

Another positive that she hadn't expected was the ability to feel Agnes's love for her family. That evening, Maggie and Logan came to take her downstairs. As they entered the room she felt a surge of affection as strong as if it had been Katy or Jack.

Logan crossed the room and took Anita's hand. "Grandmother, Maggie tells me ye want to come down to the great hall this evening and then maybe go to Mass with us."

Anita squeezed his hand and nodded.

"Ye're sure ye wouldn't rather stay here and rest?"

Anita glanced past him to Maggie who smiled indulgently at her husband's back. Anita smiled. She understood. She suspected Logan hadn't wanted Agnes to overextend herself and perhaps had argued with his wife over this. Anita looked him directly in the eye, squeezed his hand tighter and nodded again. "Ahhyyyye." The word came out as more of a groan, but he understood.

He glanced backwards towards Maggie.

Anita nearly laughed aloud at the expression on the young woman's face. She couldn't have said *I told you so* more clearly if she'd shouted it at the top of her lungs. She turned towards the wardrobe. "I'll find ye something appropriate to wear."

Logan sighed, turning back to Anita. "Then if that is what ye truly wish, I shall carry ye down. Maggie's prepared quite a throne for ye."

Maggie removed a garment from the wardrobe, helped Anita to a sitting position and helped her don a dark green woolen gown that opened in the front. Laces held it together from neck to waist. The white garment Maggie called a *léine* was visible at the neck, wrists and in front from waist to floor. Then Maggie wrapped a beautiful, soft wool blanket around her shoulders.

Once Anita was dressed, Logan slipped his arms under her knees and behind her shoulders, lifting her in one smooth motion as if she weighed no more than a child. He carried her out of the room and down the spiral staircase into the great hall.

When Anita had arrived, in the middle of Agnes's stroke, she had barely taken in her surroundings. Now she could look at leisure. It was everything she'd imagined a medieval great hall at Christmas would be. There were two large hearths, fires ablaze, at either end of the room. A large wooden table stood near one of them. Trestle tables, consisting of long boards supported on either end by something that resembled saw-horses, were being assembled in the center of the hall and benches placed on either side. A flurry of other activity suggested that they were preparing to serve a meal. The walls were hung with tapestries. Boughs of evergreen and holly adorned doors, windows, mantles and pillars. Torches set in brackets on the walls suffused the room with equal parts light and shadow.

However, Anita couldn't possibly have imagined the cacophony of smells she encountered. The pleasant scent of wood smoke and fir boughs blended with the sharper aromas of burning tallow, wet fur and sweat, unmasked by deodorant.

She also hadn't imagined how cold it would be. Even with the fires lit, it was frigid. She was thankful when Logan carried her to what looked a bit like a wide lounge chair, placed close enough to a hearth for her to be warmer than the rest of the room.

Maggie helped settle her on the cushions, covering her with another blanket. "Grandmother, are ye warm enough?"

Anita nodded.

Maggie smiled. "There are plenty of blankets. If ye need more, let me know. Ye mustn't let a chill sink in."

A lovely little girl came running towards them. "Can I sit on that nice chair with Great Granny? She can tell me a story."

"Me too, me too," shouted a little boy who looked to be about the same age who was right on her heels.

Logan frowned. "Edward, ye needn't shout and Ella, Great Granny isn't feeling well. It's hard for her to talk. She cannot tell ye stories."

Anita reached towards the little girl. She'd love to give her a cuddle even if she couldn't tell any stories.

Maggie squatted beside Ella. "It looks like Great Granny would like for ye to sit with her. And maybe ye and Edward can tell her a story."

Edward frowned. "I don't know any stories."

"Of course ye do." Maggie helped Ella onto the chair beside Anita. "Ye know all the stories Great Granny has told ye over the years."

"But she already knows all of them," said Edward, continuing to pout.

"Aye, she does," said Maggie. "But even though ye know all of them too, ye still like hearing them."

The boy nodded.

"Well, I suspect Great Granny does too."

"Really?" Edward cast Anita a questioning look.

She smiled and nodded.

"Yer smile's crooked, Great Granny," said Ella.

Maggie laid a hand on the little girl's shoulder. "Ella, ye know how Da said Great Granny isn't feeling well?"

Ella nodded.

"Well she is very, very weak, especially on the left side of her body. Which is yer left side?"

Ella raised her right hand, frowned and then raised her left hand.

"That's correct. Her left leg is weak and her left hand is weak. Even the left side of her face is weak."

"So she can only smile with her right side?" asked Edward.

Maggie smiled, obviously pleased that they had understood so well. "Aye, Edward."

The boy scrunched up his face, as if trying to smile with only half of it.

Anita chuckled, causing both children to grin.

Edward launched into story after story. They were soon joined by Evan and Malina, all four children jumping in to provide details they felt were important.

As the children talked and laughed, once again Anita felt a sense of overwhelming love for them, which must surely be her link with Agnes.

As the evening grew late, first Ella, then Edward nodded off—Ella in Anita's lap and Edward curled up next to Anita's legs. At one point, Anita herself might have dozed, but she woke as the children were lifted away from her.

Maggie knelt beside her. "Grandmother, are ye certain ye wish to go to Mass? Perhaps it would be better if ye returned to bed and rested."

Anita shook her head. Part of her wished that she could be experiencing this in a stronger, healthier body, but she didn't want to miss anything. "Maasss."

Maggie gave her a warm smile, "If that's what ye wish. I'm just going to add a few furs to yer covers. It's a bitter night and the chapel will be cold."

When Maggie had finished, the only uncovered skin was Anita's face.

Logan, Maggie and Lady Davina walked beside her as two men carried the litter out of the great hall and down the steps. Everyone else fell in behind them.

Maggie hadn't exaggerated. When the first gust of icy wind hit Anita's face, it nearly took her breath away. She smiled to herself. As a native of south Florida, it was a cold day if she had to wear socks. But thanks to Maggie, Anita was cozy in her cocoon of blankets and fur.

Snow was thick on the ground, muting the sounds of footsteps. Although the snow still fell lightly, the sky was clearing and the moon's pale light was reflected on the glistening white blanket. The members of the clan began to sing a beautiful carol about the Blessed Virgin as they walked. Although Anita had never heard these words, she recognized the haunting melody as *Creator of the Stars of Night*. She knew it was an ancient melody and it had always been one of her favorites.

In this moment, everything was so very beautiful Anita couldn't stop a tear that trickled down her cheek, blending with the melting snowflakes.

Logan's brows drew together. "Is something wrong, Grandmother? Maggie, are ye sure this was a good idea?"

Anita shook her head. She wanted to say that this was the most peaceful, beautiful Christmas Eve she'd ever experienced. But the only word she managed to form was, "Prreetty."

The laird of Clan Carr gave her a tender smile and gently brushed the tear from her cheek. "Aye, Grandmother. It's very pretty."

Mass—the Mass of the Angels they called it—was equally as beautiful. It reminded her of the Latin Masses she remembered from childhood. When it had ended, she allowed Maggie to put her to bed.

Once alone, Maggie spoke to her in English. "Did you enjoy the Mass? It's so different to what I was used to, but I do love it."

"It was lovely. I'm old enough to remember the Tridentine Mass and it brought back memories. Do you miss it much? The twenty-first century, I mean?"

"Most of the time I don't. On Christmas Eve I miss *Silent Night* and *Joy to the World*. I miss books. I *really* miss books. You know, curling up on a rainy day with an old friend like one of the *Harry Potter* series."

"I love the *Harry Potter* books too. And I'm a big fan of the movies. I can hardly wait until the next one comes out this summer. But I guess you wouldn't have seen them."

Maggie frowned, "But—" a knock at the door interrupted her. "We'll talk more tomorrow," she whispered before calling, "come in," in Gaelic.

Logan and Freya entered the room.

Logan walked to the bed and kissed Anita's cheek. "I just wanted to wish ye a good night, Grandmother."

Anita touched his cheek with her right hand. "Niiiiiight."

"'Tis very late. I'll say good night too, Grandmother." Maggie kissed her cheek. "Freya will stay with ye in case ye need anything."

Anita nodded.

"And Freya, call me if ye need me."

"Aye, my lady."

When Maggie and Logan left, Freya settled into the chair next to the bed and took Anita's hand in hers. "I'll be right here. Ye need only squeeze my hand if ye need anything at all, my lady."

Anita nodded and squeezed the young woman's hand before closing her eyes. Truthfully, she was exhausted.

As she relaxed into sleep, images of Christmases when she was a girl flitted through her mind. Her parents had always made things so wonderful. She was an only child— not by design, simply by sad chance. Her parents were married the year after her dad returned from serving in Europe in World War II and her mother became pregnant almost immediately. They wanted a big family but it wasn't to be. As far as she knew, her mother never conceived again. It was possible that she had miscarriages, but that wasn't the sort of thing her mother ever spoke about. But because of this, they considered Anita their miracle and lavished their attention on her. Christmases were particularly magical.

They became the Three Musketeers. She remained close to them their whole lives. It wasn't that long ago that she had lost them. *Oh, Agnes, if you can, tell them how much I miss them.* With that thought she drifted to sleep.

Chapter 5

When Anita woke the next morning it had once again been to the realization that she was helpless. She had lost control of her bladder in the night and was wet and chilled. She had to be washed and dressed like a child. This was harder than she'd imagined. But then Logan carried her down to the great hall where Maggie helped make her comfortable on her litter, and as the day progressed, she knew everything she suffered was absolutely worth it.

She hadn't awakened for the early morning Mass of the Shepherds, but went with the family and clan to the Mass of the Divine Word later in the morning. The morning was clear and the sun made the deep blanket of snow glitter. She had her first look at the castle in daylight and was awed. It looked like something from a fairytale. She tried to burn the image into her memory because she was certain she'd never see anything like it again.

When they returned to the great hall after Mass, the celebration started with a huge, lavish feast. Her family surrounded her, seeing to her slightest need. Logan was at her side much of the day as were Davina, Maggie and the children. There had also been a constant stream of Agnes's friends who entertained her and reminisced with her.

When the feast was cleared, minstrels entertained and the dancing started. They moved Anita's litter so she could see everything. Even though she couldn't speak—in fact she could barely move—it didn't matter. She was simply present, soaking it all in, making memories. The laughter, the singing, the crackling of the fire, the flickering candlelight. The aromas of roasted boar, hot spiced wine and fresh bread. The feel of a friendly hand holding hers or a sleeping child curled close. It was a glorious Christmas celebration, unlike any Anita had ever experienced.

Nor will I ever have this again. A lump rose in her throat at that thought.

As she pondered this, she realized it wasn't precisely true. Yes, she'd never be here, in this castle, with these people again. But perhaps the joy she felt came from being fully present, being immersed in the experience. She smiled to herself. She had no choice. Nothing kept one in the present quite as much as immobility.

She stroked the little head in her lap. She loved holding a sleeping child almost more than anything else. But try as she might, she couldn't remember a time last Christmas when she simply sat and held one of her grandchildren. Her focus had been elsewhere.

A tear slipped down her cheek. *So this wasn't all for Agnes, was it, Gertrude?*

~ * ~

The hour grew late and Maggie had chivied her children off to bed. When they were all kissed and tucked, she returned to the hall. Anita had been dozing off and on for the last hour. Maggie knew she needed to go to bed too.

She crossed the hall to the fire near which the litter had been placed. Anita was awake, but weariness was overtaking her. Maggie sat next to her. "Did ye enjoy the feast?"

Anita nodded, her eyes bright and filled with happiness.

"I'm so glad. It has been a wonderful day—one I'll never forget."

"Meee...too," Anita answered with great effort.

"Good. Now, I think it's time to help ye to bed."

Anita nodded.

"Logan, my love, Grandmother is tired. Will ye help me get her upstairs?"

"Of course, sweetling." His smile was as broad as ever, but there was sadness in his eyes. He adored Agnes. Losing her someday was inevitable but Maggie knew it didn't make facing the loss any easier. He gently lifted the tiny body of his wizened grandmother in his arms and carried her up the stairs.

Several serving women made to follow them, but Davina put up a hand. "Stay and enjoy the celebration. Maggie and I will help Lady Agnes to bed."

Logan laid his grandmother on her bed before kissing her cheek. "I love ye very much, Grandmother. Sleep well."

Anita smiled and squeezed his hand.

Logan turned to Maggie. "Are ye sure ye don't need me?"

Davina answered. "Nay son, we can manage this."

"Good night, then." He squeezed his grandmother's hand again and left.

When he was gone, Maggie said, "Anita, ye can feel free to speak English if ye wish. I'll continue to speak Gaelic so Davina can understand."

Anita smiled with the right side of her face. "Thank you so much, Maggie. This day has truly been extraordinary."

"'Tis rather different than modern Christmases. Agnes's stroke has sorely limited your ability to truly enjoy the festivities. I wish ye'd been able to experience our celebration more fully."

"Oh my precious girl, as odd as it sounds, I think it might have been perfect. Exactly what I needed."

"Ye're kidding me."

"I'm not kidding. It's all in one's perspective. Gertrude reminded me of that when she gave me the watch. Had I not been in Agnes's body I'd have seen it just the same as you. How could this," she motioned to her limp left side, "be a blessing?"

"A fair question, if ye ask me."

"But, from this perspective, I learned something. Being in this frail body meant that I had to be still and simply experience everything going on around me. I realized that at home, I am so focused on *doing* that I forget life is happening all around me. As a result, I sometimes miss what is truly important. Today I had no choice and I wouldn't have traded a single precious moment."

Maggie smiled and explained what Anita had said to Davina.

A look of wonder crossed Davina's face. "Oh my, that's…that's…"

Maggie laughed. "That's Gertrude."

Anita nodded. "My thoughts exactly. I suppose my mission has been accomplished."

"I suppose it has been." Maggie's brow drew together. "I'm sure ye're ready to return home and I know how very difficult it is for ye to be trapped in Agnes's failing body. The remainder of the celebration will be subdued, but it's more than enough that ye were here for Christmas Day."

Anita frowned. "The *rest* of the celebration?"

"Aye. Unlike Christmas in our time, where everyone rushes out to take advantage of sales on the day after Christmas, here we celebrate the entire twelve days, right through to Epiphany."

Anita sighed. "I knew that, I guess I'd forgotten. I thought I'd only be here for a couple days."

"And so ye were. Ye've given us a great gift as it is. I won't ask for more."

"No, Maggie. Now that I think about it, Gertrude asked me to stay for the 'Christmas Season' and I agreed. I won't break my promise. It's fairly clear Gertrude has a plan and maybe the mission isn't accomplished yet. I'll see it through. It's just a little less than two weeks. I can do this."

"Are ye certain?"

"Yes. Absolutely."

Maggie wasn't sure why, but she felt a great sense of relief at that and it was more than just having Agnes present for the benefit of her family. Agnes was gone and she had accepted that and soon the family would as well. Maggie knew this wasn't about Agnes at all. Maggie had to admit, if only to herself, she wasn't ready for *Anita* to go, but she wasn't sure why.

Normally, it would be her inclination to try to spare someone from unnecessary suffering if she could. Anita was locked in Agnes's failing body with all the pain and indignities that came with that. For Anita to stay twelve more days was a huge sacrifice. Maggie would never have asked it of her. Still, the fact remained that she wanted Anita to stay—just a little longer. She couldn't exactly put her finger on why this was so important to her yet, but she was tired. She'd worry about it tomorrow.

~ * ~

When Anita awoke the next day, snow was falling. Logan tried valiantly to convince his grandmother to stay in bed and rest today.

"Naaay," was all Anita could manage to say. She'd read about St. Stephen's day in a book once and knew that animals were blessed as part of the celebration. She wanted to see that. And she wanted to see the snow falling.

Maggie laid a hand on Logan's arm. "Logan, this is important to Grandmother. I swear, I'll see that she takes a long rest this afternoon before tonight's feast."

So once again, Anita was bundled up on her litter and carried to the church. The snow fell heavily. She had never experienced a snowfall and was surprised at the way it *sounded*. Noises were muted and that made sense when she thought about it. But she hadn't expected to *hear* the snow falling. There was the faintest *tick, tick, tick*, as the tiny icy flakes landed.

During Mass the priest blessed hay, salt and oats. Anita would have to ask Maggie about this later. After Mass, the priest led a procession to the stables, where he blessed the horses.

Anita smiled to herself as she watched. Maggie seemed to love the great beasts. She remembered how much Katy had loved horses as a teenager and suspected Maggie had been no different.

When the ceremonies were over, just as she'd promised, Maggie insisted that *Grandmother* return to bed. "I'll sit with ye while ye rest. 'Twill be another late night."

She shooed everyone else out of the room, then sat beside Anita. "I hope you don't mind. We've had no time alone and I want to hear about your life and how Gertrude came to offer you the pocket watch."

"I've wondered about your story as well. But first I have a question. I gather that St. Stephen is a patron of animals."

"That's right. And the blessed hay, salt and oats will be distributed to our farmers and given to sick animal through the year."

"I always think of St. Francis as the patron of animals."

Maggie laughed. "I do too, but here, St Francis is still a relatively new saint. It's only been a little over fifty years since he died and was canonized. How crazy is that? *St. Francis was eighteen when Agnes was born.* And St Catherine of Siena hasn't even been born yet. When I stop and think about things like that, it amazes me even after all these years."

"Tell me about yourself, I mean who you were."

"My name was Magdalena Mitchell. I lived near Trenton, New Jersey with my dad. He was a physics professor at Princeton."

"And how did you meet Gertrude?"

"It's a long story, but she found me sobbing in a sculpture garden on a beautiful June day."

"Why were you crying?"

"The man I thought I loved had just married someone else."

"Oh dear. How did that happen?"

"I won't bore you with all the details, but I'd delayed going to school and pursuing my dreams because my mother was diagnosed with cancer when I was a senior in high school. I stayed home to help her and my family and he went on without me."

"Your poor mother. Were they able to treat the cancer? Did she recover?"

A shadow of loss crossed Maggie's face. "No. It was too advanced when she was diagnosed."

"I'm so very sorry, sweetheart."

"Thank you. I miss her. I always will." Maggie looked pensive for a moment before continuing. "Anyway, Gertrude gave me the watch when I said I wished I could have someone else's life. Boy was I surprised when I arrived over seven hundred years in the past."

"Gertrude didn't tell you where you were coming?"

"No. I gather she told you, because you knew about Agnes and the stroke."

"Yes she did. I can't imagine the shock of landing here with no clue where or *when* you were."

"That's putting it mildly. But it didn't take me long to realize this is where my destiny was. I belonged here."

"And ye've been here for eleven years?"

Maggie nodded.

Eleven years? But Maggie said she enjoyed the Harry Potter *books*—plural—and only the first one had been released eleven years ago. *How can that be?*

Before Anita could sort it out, Maggie said, "Tell me about yourself. Where are you from?"

"I live in southwest Florida with my husband and I was a teacher. I used to teach sixth grade."

"Used to?"

"I'm fifty-eight and I retired a couple years ago."

"Is that when you moved to Florida?"

Anita laughed. "No. We've actually always lived in Florida."

"Do you have children?"

"We have a son and a daughter. Our son is thirty. He's married and has two daughters—three year old Lucy, and Olivia who's one."

"What's your son's name?"

"John James Lewis. It's my husband's name and was his father's name too. My father-in-law was always called 'John' and my husband was 'James' or 'Jim'. So when we gave our son the name, we decided to call him Jack."

"And your daughter?"

"She's twenty-seven and her name is Katy. They both live in the Washington, DC area."

"Why so far from home?"

"They went to school in the northeast and that's where they found jobs. Jack is a patent attorney and works for the US patent and trademark office. Katy has a degree in computer science from Georgetown."

"You're kidding. My old boyfriend, the one I was crying about when Gertrude gave me the watch, got his computer science degree from Georgetown."

"Really? When did he graduate?"

"In twenty-twelve."

Anita was stunned. "What did you say?"

"He graduated in twenty-twelve."

"But…wait, I don't understand. When did Gertrude give you the pocket watch?"

"In June of twenty-fourteen."

Anita couldn't get her head around it. Maggie was from farther in the future than Anita herself was. That meant…that meant *Maggie hadn't left yet* in her time.

"What's wrong?" asked Maggie.

"Nothing. I just assumed, since you've been here for more than eleven years, you used the watch more than eleven years ago."

"I did."

Anita looked at her. "No you didn't. *You haven't used it yet.* Gertrude gave me the watch in December two thousand and eight. When I go back, you'll still be there."

Maggie's mouth fell open in shock. "*Two thousand eight?* I never imagined…but I'm not sure why I'm surprised. Gertrude said time is not linear and she seems to pop back and forth at will."

"When was your mother diagnosed with cancer?"

"Two thousand and nine."

"Not until next year for me. Maggie, if I find her when I go back, maybe I can talk her into getting checked out sooner. Maybe they can find it earlier and it won't take her life."

For a moment Maggie just stared at Anita, stunned. Then her face lit with excitement. "You're right. You can warn her. They could catch the cancer a year earlier and maybe…maybe…"

The joy which seemed to have filled Maggie, dissipated as quickly as it came. Maggie shook her head sadly. "No, you can't."

"Of course I could. There is a way."

Maggie smiled at her. "I can't imagine what my life would have been like if she hadn't died. Those years were incredibly hard and I miss her so much. Part of me is sorely tempted, even if only for my dad and sister. But if I've learned nothing else, it's that the universe unfolds as it should. My life happened as it did for a reason and I am blissfully happy here. I'm not even sure you even *could* change it if you tried. I know this may seem crazy to you, but my mother's illness and everything surrounding it has already happened. Even though two thousand and nine is your future, it's my past. And then there's always the chance that attempting to change even the smallest thing could make the entire situation worse. As hard as those years were, I made it through them and landed here. This is my life now. I wouldn't change it for anything."

Anita nodded. "I guess I understand. As a mother, it breaks my heart to know what's ahead for your younger self. I wish I could do something for you, even if just to make things easier somehow, but I understand."

"Thank you, Anita." Maggie took hold of Anita's hands, giving her a thoughtful look. "But maybe there is something you can do to help me after all. I have a past that I can't share with my present and a present that I can't share with my past."

"I'm not sure I understand."

"As I told ye no one but Logan and Davina know I'm a time-traveler. I will never be able to tell my children about their grandparents or their Aunt Paige. I can't tell them stories from my childhood or any fond memories."

"Ah, I understand, *a past you can't share with your present*. And you can't share your new family with your old one."

"Exactly. But maybe you can. I used the pocket watch on the twenty-first of June, two thousand fourteen. Maybe someday, after that date, you can look up my sister, Paige. I did tell her about the Pocket Watch before I left and she knows who Gertrude is. She'll believe you. You can tell her all about my life here. Tell her about my children, my husband, Davina and Agnes, and my clan. Tell her how much I love and miss her but also how very happy I am."

"I certainly can do that. I'll find her. I promise. But over the next few days, you need to tell me everything you can about the last eleven years. So I'll write down everything

I can remember when I get home. Then I'll have plenty to tell her."

For the next eleven days, through all of the celebrations, Anita and Maggie made time to be alone every day. Anita got a glimpse of medieval life unlike anything she could ever learn from a book as Maggie told her about her life. But they also talked about things from their lives in the twenty-first century.

Maggie shared her past. She reminisced about Christmases when she was little. She laughed about school concerts, cookie baking disasters and Christmas pageants. "I don't think this season ever passes that I don't think about *A Miracle on 34th Street*, *It's a Wonderful Life* or *The Grinch*. When I was little I always imagined watching them with my children the way my Mom and Dad did with me and Paige."

"Still, by everything I've seen, no one here has lost sight of the real meaning of Christmas."

Maggie smiled. "No. You are right in that. I hadn't thought of it that way."

They also shared their mutual love of books—Harry Potter being a topic they both loved. "But I won't tell you how it ends, so don't bother asking," Maggie had told her one afternoon.

The days between Christmas and Epiphany fairly flew, even though Anita felt the strain of Agnes's failing body more and more each day.

The final feast, on Epiphany, was spectacular. This was the day the Carrs exchanged gifts and it felt very like Christmas Day in Anita's own time. She wasn't sure how it had happened, but in these few short days, she had come to love each of them as if they were her own and being with them gave her joy. She realized she would miss them. She'd miss them quite a lot.

As Anita went to sleep that night it occurred to her that she didn't have to leave yet. She could stay for the full time allowed by the pocket watch and still return home on Christmas Eve.

Chapter 6

Monday, January 7, 1282
Castle Carr

The day after Epiphany dawned gray and cold. The wind carried a damp chill and wet snow started falling before noon. This was the first morning since arriving in medieval Scotland that Anita could not face leaving Agnes's bed.

The fire in her hearth blazed, warming the chamber as much as possible, but leaving the bed to use the chamber pot had been a miserably cold experience. It took piles of blankets and furs to banish the chill. And nothing could stop her body from aching. Every single joint pained her and it was impossible to get comfortable.

Maggie sat beside Anita, helping her eat warm, sweet porridge, but after a few bites, Anita shook her head. "Nooo. Nooo mohr." Anita spoke Gaelic as Freya was still in the room.

"It's all right, Grandmother. Maybe ye'll feel like more later. Freya, will ye take this tray back to the kitchen please?"

"Aye, my lady. Shall I return then and sit with Lady Agnes for a while?"

"No, I'll stay with her."

When Freya had left and the sound of her retreating footsteps had died away, Maggie took Anita's hand in hers. Tears filled her eyes. "It's time, isn't it?"

"Time to go home? I...well..." Truthfully, in spite of last night's thoughts of staying longer night, Anita did want to go home. She had experienced wonderful things here, but she was so very weary this morning. Still, part of her wasn't ready to leave quite yet. Maybe just a day or two more. "I could stay a little longer."

"I would love for you to stay longer. I know you aren't Agnes. I know she is waiting peacefully to move on. You have given my family and this clan, not to mention Agnes herself, a wonderful gift. But of everyone, I think perhaps I was most blessed by your presence here. It's as if I've had a visitor from home. I love my life here, but even though Davina and Logan know who I am, they cannot understand what life in our time was like. I loved being able to talk about books and movies and music with you. It was a priceless Christmas present which I shall never forget."

Anita understood this. Having no shared past must come with a certain amount of loneliness. Then too, Maggie was a lot like Katy. Anita had grown to love her and the realization that she would never see her or be able to talk to her again caused Anita's heart to break. "I'm not sure I'm ready to leave you yet."

The tears that had been swimming in Maggie's eyes slipped down her cheeks as she tightened her grip on Anita's hand. "And I don't think I'll ever be ready for you to leave. But, Anita, the gifts you've given us have taken their toll."

A knock sounded at the door. Maggie frowned and swiped at the tears on her face. "Come in."

The door opened and an elderly woman in a black cloak entered.

"*Gertrude*," both Maggie and Anita said in unison.

Maggie crossed the room and hugged the old woman.

Gertrude smiled broadly. "Good morning, ladies. I trust you've had a blessed Christmas season?"

"*Blessed?*" Anita smiled the crooked smile she was getting used to. "Yes, Gertrude, that describes it perfectly." Anita sighed heavily. She was so very tired.

Maggie smiled broadly. "Thank you, Gertrude. Thank you for everything."

"'Twas my pleasure, and I am so glad things went well."

"We were just talking about when Anita should go home. I hate to see her leave—"

"But her time is up."

Maggie shook her head, frowning. "No. She arrived on Christmas Eve. It's only been fourteen days."

Gertrude caressed Maggie's cheek with her wrinkled hand. "Sadly, there is a different clock ticking. Agnes's body is failing. She would have died on Christmas Eve or within a day or two had Anita, with her determination and stamina, not taken up residence. But this frail earthly shell has very little time left. The universe is unfolding as it should. Goodbyes must be said and Anita needs to say her word, while she can."

Maggie gasped and ran to the door. She called to someone in the hall. "Please, run get the Laird and Lady Davina. Quickly. Lady Agnes has taken a turn." Then she came back to the bed. "Before anyone else gets here, Anita, thank you, it's very little but it's all I have. I love you."

"I love you too, sweet girl. Take care of your wonderful family. I'll never forget you." As soon as the words were out, she knew she only had energy for one more.

Davina was there almost immediately. She went to the bedside, took Anita's hand, and whispered, "Thank you, Anita. God be with you, always."

Logan burst into the room moments later, looking as if he had run flat out from where ever he'd been. He knelt by her bed and put his arms around her. "Grandmother, I love you."

With great effort, Anita raised her right hand enough to touch his cheek before whispering, "*Flamingo.*"

~ * ~

Anita gasped and sat up. She was in her own bed, in her own time. She was able to move and the pain that she'd lived with for days was gone. She glanced at the clock. Although she wasn't certain of the exact time she'd fallen asleep, she knew it had been just after midnight. It was still only minutes after twelve.

Jim roused slightly from sleep. "Something wrong?"

Anita wrapped her arms around him and kissed him. "No. Nothing's wrong. I just had a dream. Go back to sleep."

He rolled over onto his side and in a moment was snoring loudly again.

Anita smiled at him, climbed out of bed and went to the bathroom. She shut the door and turned on the light.

The light. A flip of a switch and the bathroom was brilliantly illuminated. Light bouncing off all of the chrome and porcelain fixtures.

And the toilet. *Oh you beautiful toilet.* Two weeks of being unable to control her bodily functions—and even when she could a chamber pot being the only convenience available—made modern plumbing seem nothing short of luxurious.

She laughed aloud as she turned to look at her own reflection in the mirror. So much had happened to her it hardly seemed possible that it didn't show. She felt a bit like she expected Ebenezer Scrooge had felt after his remarkable night with the ghosts of Christmases Past, Present and Future. It was nearly impossible to believe almost no time had passed and it was still only the wee hours of the morning on Christmas Eve.

It had been the most extraordinary experience of her life but as she knew it would, her heart already ached for Maggie and the rest of the Carrs. "But they lived hundreds of years ago. Even the children, Evan, Malina, Elasaid, Edward and little Maretta, have now grown old and returned to dust," she told her reflection. *No.* She refused to think of it that way. What had Maggie said? *Time is not linear.* That means time can loop on itself. *They are simply elsewhere.* And for that matter, sixteen-year-old Magdalena Mitchell was tucked snuggly in her bed in New Jersey, a wonderful Christmas ahead of her with her parents and sister.

"And you have a wonderful Christmas ahead too," she told herself, smiling wryly as she remembered what she'd told Gertrude in the mall. *"If being alone on Christmas Eve is a gift, where do I return it?"*

Gertrude had indeed fixed Christmas by adjusting Anita's perspective on things. Time with her children and grandchildren was priceless, no matter when they arrived.

Anita returned to bed. With her heart and mind so full of all she had experienced, she was certain she'd never fall asleep. But to the contrary, she drifted off quickly.

Chapter 7

Normally Anita was only vaguely aware of Jim's alarm going off as it did every morning at six. She usually slept until seven-thirty or eight after that before starting her day. But this morning her mind was on the Carrs and even as tired as she felt, she had trouble going back to sleep after it went off and Jim had dressed and left for the day. It was still hard to believe she had experienced all of that in the space of seconds last night. Then her thoughts turned to Maggie—how Anita wished she could reach out to the girl. But Maggie had been right, the Maggie she became doesn't exist yet and wouldn't if Anita did anything to interfere. Her heart ached to know the pain and loss that was in store for the girl. But as Maggie had said, attempting to change even the smallest thing could make the entire situation worse and those few hard years were a small price for the life she'd gained.

Eventually Anita must have dozed off because she woke to Jim nudging her. She was immediately awake. "What's wrong? What time is it? Did something happen at work?"

"Everything is fine. I'm not working today."

"Yesterday, on the phone, you said you had to work today."

"No, I said, if we didn't get things sorted we'd have to work late today. But, we stayed a little later yesterday so we could get to a stopping point. I gave the whole crew the day off today. We don't start up again until Monday."

"Wow. That's great." There had been many years—years when the kids were small and there was loads still to do—when having Jim home all day on Christmas Eve would have been a life-saver. "But wait a minute, you got up and left. Where did you go?"

"I had a few errands to run."

She smiled. He was famous for waiting until the last minute to get Christmas presents. "You went shopping at six-thirty? I guess that's one way to beat the crowds. Still, there can't have been much open."

"The stores I needed were open this morning."

"So are you finished? Or do you have shopping still?"

"I don't have shopping, but I do have plans for the day."

"That's okay. Everything is pretty much done here so go do what you've planned. I guess I'll make the crab soup, then watch Christmas movies and crochet."

"No can do. My plans involve you."

"They do?" She sat up in bed, waiting to hear them.

He smirked. "Yeah they do."

"Are you going to tell me what they are?"

"Not yet. Breakfast first."

"Okay, I'll make eggs."

"No you won't. I picked up fresh squeezed orange juice, bagels, cream cheese and smoked salmon this morning."

Anita smiled. "That's nice." Jim loved bagels and salmon. It wasn't her absolute favorite but she liked it well enough too.

He grinned. "I got strawberry cream cheese too."

"Now that sounds perfect."

When they'd eaten the bagels and Jim sat finishing his coffee, Anita stood, leaned down and kissed him. "Thanks for the orange juice and bagels, honey, they were a really nice surprise." She carried the dirty dishes to the sink.

He waggled his eyebrows. "That's only the start."

"So what's next on your agenda?"

"Go put on a bathing suit."

"Why?"

"The weather is supposed to be great today. We're going to the beach."

Anita was flabbergasted. "The beach? You don't like the beach."

"That's not true. I don't like sitting on the beach for hours doing nothing. But I like walking on the beach with you, and I like fishing while you relax on the beach and read. It's been a while since we've taken the boat out. I thought we'd go to Cayo Costa for the day."

"You're kidding." Cayo Costa was an island state park only accessible by boat and it was one of Anita's favorite places. But even though they lived on a canal with access to the Gulf, their boat spent much more time on the lift than it did in the water. They always seemed too busy.

"I'm not kidding. The weather is perfect. I picked up subs, snacks and drinks from Publix and I've already stashed them in the cooler, on board. The towels, chairs, umbrella and fishing rods are all taken care of too. All you have to do is put on a swimsuit, grab a hat and get on the boat."

"Okay. I just need to get back in time to make the crab soup before we go to Mass."

"No, you don't."

"But we always have crab soup and snacks after Mass on Christmas Eve."

"We haven't always."

"Of course we have, it's our tradition."

He stood, crossed the kitchen and took her hands in his. "Anita, it has not *always* been our tradition. When your parents were still alive, before we had kids, even before we were married, we went out to dinner with them on Christmas Eve and then went to the late Mass. But when Jack was a toddler we stopped that. We went to the earlier Mass and then back to your parents' for dinner. Then, after a few years, you thought fixing both Christmas Eve and Christmas Day dinner was too much for your mom. She still wanted to have

everyone in for Christmas Day, so we started having them
over to our house on Christmas Eve. I think the first time you
fixed crab soup was when Katy was three or four. Both kids
loved it and Jack asked for it again the next year. *That's* how
it became a tradition."

"Okay, it hasn't *always* been a tradition, but it has
been for the last twenty-three years or so. And you love crab
soup."

"I know. But things are different this year. The fact is
the way we've celebrated Christmas has changed as our lives
have. Even in the last twenty-three years." He winked at her.
"Since we've had crab soup every Christmas Eve, subtle
things have changed along the way. The kids grew up and we
added a nice wine to dinner. We lost your mom and started
having both Christmas Eve and Christmas Day at our house.
We lost your dad and it was no longer three generations.
Then Jack and Erica had Lucy and it was three generations
again." He smiled. "And Santa started visiting again, only he
sounded much more like me than your dad."

She laughed.

He moved closer, gathering her in his arms. "The
constant hasn't been the food we served or the things we did
on Christmas Eve. It wasn't the presence of your parents, our
children or our grandchildren. The tradition, the only
tradition that we've had since before we were married, was
that we spend Christmas together. You and me. Each step of
the way since before our marriage, through good times and
bad, we have had each other and we still do. We had thirty
Christmas Eves with both of our children and we may have
more. But now we need to turn back to each other, where we
started. We are the constant in all of this and will be for years
to come, God willing. And even when the inevitable happens,
we still hold so much of each other in our hearts that we'll
never truly be parted."

She nestled her head against his chest as tears slipped down her cheeks. He was right. Life evolved, but they had each other through it all. "I love you, Jim."

He kissed the top of her head. "I love you too." After a moment, he took a step back and she wiped the tears from her cheeks.

He grinned. "Now, let's go start new traditions."

~ * ~

It had been a spectacular day. The temperature reached the low eighties, the humidity was low and the sky was deep cerulean blue from horizon to horizon. A few puffy clouds appeared in the early afternoon. When the breeze picked up and it became a little cloudier later in the afternoon, they packed up and went home.

After they'd put everything away and the boat was on the lift and had been hosed down, Anita glanced at her watch. "We've missed Christmas Eve Mass at our parish. I'll look and see who has a later one."

"Nope. We have dinner reservations at six-thirty. You have just enough time to shower and change."

"Dinner reservations too?" It was rarely Jim's idea to eat out, especially not during the snow-bird season when everything was crowded.

"I thought it might be nice. After dinner we can come home, put our feet up, have a drink and maybe watch a movie…or something."

"Are you planning to go to a midnight Mass somewhere?"

"Nope. I plan to be in bed by midnight. I thought we could have a leisurely breakfast in the morning, go to the last Mass and then make a pot of crab soup when we get home."

"Crab soup for Christmas dinner?"

"Why not? I've been thinking about it. Jack and Erica's flight is due in at four. With getting luggage and all, it'll be nearly five before we get home. The kids will be tired.

Let's just treat it like we used to do Christmas Eve—a light supper, an elf gift for the kids and an early night. We can leave presents and roast beef until the next day. That way Katy will be sure to be here."

Anita was flabbergasted. He had every detail planned. "How long have you been thinking about this? Ever since Jack said they wouldn't be here until Christmas Day?"

He chuckled and pulled her into a hug. "No, baby. When I called yesterday it was just to ask if you wanted me to go straight to the airport to pick Katy up, or if you wanted me to swing by and get you first. But I knew you were really upset about it, so I made a command decision. I told you I was working late, then as soon as I was off the phone, I told the crew. There were a few grumbles until I told them we could all have Christmas Eve off if we just worked a few more hours into the evening. I didn't want you to be alone today."

"And that's when you decided to do all this?"

"Does that sound like me?"

"No."

He laughed. "Smart girl. I forgot to turn my alarm off last night. When it went off, I decided to get up and go get bagels. Then on my way back from the bagel shop, I was driving past Publix and remembered how much fun it was to take a picnic out on the boat, so I stopped to get subs. It was strictly a plan by the seat of my pants day."

"When did you make the dinner reservations?"

"When you were changing into your swimsuit."

"And the idea of pushing things out a day? Crab soup tomorrow and Christmas dinner the next day?"

"Well, I'll admit, I had that idea weeks ago. But I figured I'd wait until Katy was here to propose it."

They went to their favorite Italian restaurant for dinner and it was as wonderful as ever. When they got home after dinner, Anita turned the tree lights on and lit some candles while Jim busied himself in the kitchen.

Anita called, "What movie do you want to watch?"

"*A Charlie Brown Christmas.*"

"You're kidding."

"Nope. I like it. I was probably fifteen or sixteen when it first came out and I thought I was too old for it. So I think the first time I actually watched was when Jack was little."

"Okay. We have the DVD here somewhere. She found it and put it into the player.

He walked into the family room with highball glasses filled with a brown liquid.

"What's in the glasses?"

"Another new tradition. Instead of hot spiced cider or perked punch, drinks that we've always made in spite of the warm weather, I just invented a latitude-appropriate Christmas beverage. I'm going to call it *Florida spiced cider*. I sweetened fresh cider with caramel sauce and added a dash of orange juice."

"Where does the spice come in?"

"That would be the healthy shot of spiced rum." He kissed her and handed her one of the drinks.

Anita laughed. "Sounds delicious."

They curled up together on the couch and she pushed "play" on the remote. "I don't think I've watched this in years."

"Honey, I think the kids watch it every Christmas Eve."

"I know it's been on. I just don't think I've taken the time to sit down and watch it in ages."

"That's because you were too busy making crab soup."

Anita frowned. He wasn't being critical, but it was true. Part of her "traditional Christmas Eve" was the flurry of work she did to prepare everything. She didn't usually sit down and relax until after the dishes were done and she was usually exhausted by the time she fell into bed. It was the good kind of exhaustion. The kind one feels when they've accomplished a great deal and are both happy and proud of the results. But still, it was exhaustion.

She thought about the medieval celebrations with the Carrs. Of course a tremendous amount of work had been required to prepare for them. She suspected that had Lady Agnes not been infirm, she too would have bustled around a bit, doing what she could. It was only because of the stroke that Anita, as Lady Agnes, could simply rest and take it all in. Maggie and Davina had intentionally taken time away from the work, to *make memories*. It was only in stopping and absorbing everything going on around them that they could make memories. Maybe that was why many of Anita's memories, the things she *thought* were the important traditions were things she did *for* the family instead of *with* the family. But it wasn't baking cookies or making crab soup or putting Christmas dinner on the table that had been the important part of their traditions. Looking back now, she realized her strongest, dearest memories were of the time she spent with her family. The date on the calendar really didn't matter. They would have many more wonderful times together.

She sipped on her drink and watched Charlie Brown with Jim. She had to smile as she saw way too much of Lucy van Pelt in herself.

And then, Linus spoke, reciting the Christmas story, and she remembered snuggling up on the couch and watching it with Jack and Katy when they were small. More precisely, she remembered watching them watch it. The expressions on their faces when Linus spoke in the quiet auditorium. The indescribable cuteness, when they were a little older and imitated the carolers—their eyes closed, lips in the shape of a perfect "O", taking an exaggerated breath at the end of each phrase. Memory making at its finest.

That was the thing about making memories: one had to be there, in the present, absorbing everything.

When the Peanuts' gang yelled, "Merry Christmas, Charlie Brown," Jim kissed her head and whispered, "Merry Christmas, Anita."

"Merry Christmas, Jim." She raised her nearly empty glass. "And here's to new traditions and making new memories."

"Here, here." He clinked his glass against hers before draining it.

"It's still early. Do you want to watch another movie?"

"Nope. There is another new tradition I want to try." He got up, walked to the tree, pulled a package from under it, and brought it to her. "It's an elf gift."

Anita laughed. "Elf gifts are not a new tradition." The elves stopped by the house every Christmas Eve, while they were at Mass, and left a present for each kid. Oddly enough, the present was always new pajamas that had already been washed once and were ready to wear. As the kids grew older, the elves started leaving something for Mom and Dad too. Slippers, robes or even tee-shirts were common.

Jim nodded, looking very serious. "Well, technically yes, but this year the present is for both of us from a very naughty elf." He handed her the package. "But you can unwrap it."

Curious, Anita tore the paper off, opened the box and started giggling. She pulled out a sexy, deep red babydoll. "Cute, honey. But there's nothing in the box for you."

"Oh, I beg to differ. You go put that on, and *then* I get to unwrap my present."

Anita grinned. "You're on." She headed to the bedroom, calling over her shoulder, "I'll be ready by the time you turn off the lights and blow out the candles."

She undressed quickly and pulled the nighty on. She was actually surprised. She had shopped for things like this before. Usually, if she could find anything in more generous sizes, they just looked kind of silly on her. This garment was well made and styled to fit a fuller figure. She looked at herself in the mirror and actually liked the way it looked.

In the mirror's reflection, she saw the bedroom door open.

Jim stood there holding one of the still-lit candles. "Now that's what I'm talking about." He turned off the light and walked up behind her, placing the candle on the dresser before wrapping his arms around her.

She continued to look in the mirror. "It's pretty. I like it."

He kissed her behind her ear. Jim's sprinkling of gray hair glowed silver in the soft flickering light. He ran his hands lightly over her belly and up to her breasts, cupping them in his hands. He kissed his way down her shoulder. "You're pretty. I like you."

She chuckled, turning in his arms to face him. "Well, your vision isn't what it used to be."

"My vision is perfect." He swatted her backside lightly before cupping a hand over each cheek and pulling her close. His mouth slanted across hers, kissing her, lightly at first then deeply and urgently as if he couldn't get enough.

She closed her eyes, swept away by his kiss. She loved this. She always had.

His kisses moved to her temples, her eyes, her throat. He pushed the silky fabric aside and lowered his head to one breast, kissing, sucking, nibbling. It was as if electricity shot through her, igniting her desire.

"I'm ready to unwrap my present now," he said, his voice low and throaty with desire.

She pulled his head back to her face, kissing his lips then whispering, "I have a little more unwrapping to do first." She slid her hands under his shirt, rubbing them over his chest for a moment before lifting the shirt up and pulling it over his head.

He kicked off his shoes while she unbuckled his belt. She caught her thumbs in his waistband, pushing it down and over his hips. He kicked out of his pants before capturing her mouth in another soul-stirring kiss. He rained kisses over her face and down her neck as he pushed her, ever so slowly, towards the bed. His hands ran lightly down her back until he reached the hem of the short gown. Then, just as she had, he slid his hands under the garment and up her sides, pulling it up as he went. In an instant it was over her head and discarded with his clothes on the floor.

Anita laid down on the bed, scooting to the center and reaching for him.

He tsked. "I've barely just unwrapped my gift. I want to play for a while." He made a circular motion with one hand. "Roll over."

Anita did, hugging several pillows to her chest and turning her head to one side. She closed her eyes.

He stepped away from the bed for a moment, then she felt the bed sink under his weight as he knelt beside her. He bent over her and kissed her neck, then nuzzled behind her ear, causing her to giggle. He gave a low, throaty chuckle and planted kisses slowly and deliberately down her back until he reached the ultrasensitive spot at the base of her spine.

He knelt up again. There was the unmistakable squelch of lotion being squeezed from a tube followed by Jim rubbing his hands together. A moment later, he began rubbing the lotion into her back and she was in paradise. The rough skin on his hands combined with firm, gentle pressure could not be duplicated by the most skilled massage therapist.

His hands slid under her arms, grazing the edge of her breasts before returning to her back. He massaged his way down over the base of her spine and onto her backside. He massaged her cheeks and thighs, his thumbs circling ever deeper, closer to her core. When she was panting with need he helped her turn onto her back.

He massaged and kissed her breasts, nibbling first on one then the other. "I love these. You have gorgeous breasts."

"They aren't what they used to be."

"Thank God for that." At her questioning frown he added, "If they were it would mean you weren't a mother and we'd have no children."

"Or that I had a good plastic surgeon."

He brushed his thumbs over her nipples, causing them to pebble before giving them a light squeeze, eliciting a surprised gasp.

"I prefer them just like this. Soft and responsive."

He kissed his way down her belly, moving between her legs as he did. There were no words between them. They had become unnecessary years ago. When she reached the point where she could stand it no longer, he raised up on his knees and slid his hot length into her. He started moving in her, at first achingly slow. She rose to meet him, pushing him to drive harder and faster. In a moment, or perhaps an eternity, she was overcome with the shuddering waves of her climax. The muscles at her core contracted repeatedly around him until she felt the warmth of his seed filling her.

They lay like this, connected, in each other's arms as they had so many times. It was beautiful and perfect. She adored this man who knew every tiny detail about her. He had been right. They, the two of them, were the constant in a world that would continue to change around them.

Chapter 8

December 23, 2014
Hamilton, New Jersey

It had been six years since Gertrude had encouraged Anita to look at things from a different perspective and had asked her to help an old woman and her family have one last Christmas together. Those had been the most remarkable fourteen days, or rather fourteen seconds, of Anita's life. And that Christmas—the one she'd been convinced was ruined—had been equally as memorable.

Jack had arrived as planned late in the afternoon on Christmas Day. A light supper and a quiet evening was exactly what his little family needed.

Katy had called that morning to wish them Merry Christmas and tell them she hadn't been able to book a flight from Philadelphia on Christmas Day. "I am standing by for a direct flight tomorrow morning, but if that doesn't work out, I can take one later that connects through Chicago. I'll definitely be there by dinner time—as long as you don't eat too early."

But a little after seven in the evening, on Christmas Day, she arrived with her new fiancé, Anthony Soldani.

Anita could scarcely believe it. After hugs were shared all around she said, "I thought you couldn't get a single seat on a flight today, much less two. What happened?"

Katy grinned broadly. "Well, Anthony's sister-in-law—his oldest brother's wife—heard me talking to you on the phone and apparently made a few calls. By the time we sat down to dinner this afternoon she had arranged for us to fly by *private jet*."

Jim scowled. "You're kidding. Who can get a private jet on Christmas Day?"

Anthony laughed. "My sister-in-law, Elizabeth. She comes from a fairly wealthy family."

Katy shrugged. "I told her I didn't want to take the pilot away from his family today. She just laughed and said he jumped at the chance when he found out he could bring them along and have a few days at a beach resort as a surprise Christmas present."

Yes, that had been an amazing Christmas. But then, each Christmas since had been extraordinary in its own way, Anita made certain of it. She immersed herself fully into each celebration and savored the joy around her, regardless of where she was and who she was with.

When the season had passed that year, everyone had gone home and the decorations were put away, Anita realized that memories, even the best ones, could be fleeting. Even now, just days later, things were fading a bit. She had made Maggie a promise and she couldn't fulfill it if she allowed herself to forget anything.

So Anita spent days writing down every single detail that she could remember of her time as Agnes. Even after she had finished with the bulk of it, if something happening around her reminded her of a moment she hadn't captured, she'd jot it down and add it to the memoir. It had been a labor of love for a young woman who she'd hold in her heart forever. As a result her memories of those fourteen days stayed vivid and fresh.

But Anita didn't tuck the memoir away when she was finished. She kept it in her desk drawer so that she could read it from time to time. In fact, she read it often. She'd pull it out and curl up with it on a rainy day. When life seemed to be rushing by, she'd take a step back and revisit those memories. The words reawakened every tender moment for her. She was connected again through the sights, sounds and even the smells that she'd lovingly recorded. Over the years she smiled at one of the first sentences she had written: *I wish I could have had a camera*. Photos would have been nice, but putting the memories into words, even if it took thousands, had served their purpose.

The memoir resulted in a new, private tradition. Sometime, during the week before Christmas, she would find time, alone and uninterrupted, when she could read it through and savor it all again. A couple of years ago, she had dozed off while reading it in her recliner. She woke to find Jim standing next to her, reading the pages that had slipped from her hand.

Oh, dear God. She had never told him about her experience with the pocket watch.

"Wow, Anita, this is a great story. Did you write it?"

Story? Okay we can go with that. "Uh, yeah. It's nothing really. I was just fooling around a little."

"I think it's good. You might have something here. Maybe you could get it published."

Anita laughed. "I doubt it, but I'll keep it in mind."

So for the last six years, she kept the memories alive and fresh for the day when she could tell Maggie's sister everything. Anita had also kept her word about never seeking out Magdalena Mitchell. Oh, she looked her up. With the internet being what it is, she knew when Maggie graduated from high school and then nursing school. She knew when Maggie's mother Elise had died.

Oddly, life pulled Anita closer and closer to the Mitchells. As it turned out, Anthony's younger brother, Luke, taught at the Catholic high school Maggie attended. In fact, Luke had been one of her teachers. Even so, Anita never reached out.

Now, however, that was about to change. Earlier this year, on June the twenty-second, Magdalena Mitchell had passed away suddenly in the night. The time had come to share Maggie's life with her sister.

The problem was, Anita had never once imagined how she would do this. The immediate aftermath of the funeral seemed the wrong time. But when was the right time to contact a stranger and tell her about something like this?

Then Katy, Anthony and their three children were visiting at Thanksgiving and Katy asked, "Mom, how about you and Dad come to New Jersey for Christmas? Jack can drive up with his family either Christmas Eve or Christmas Day. It'll be fun. Maybe it'll be your first white Christmas."

Anita had smiled. Her first white Christmas had been at Castle Carr in Scotland, in the year twelve-eighty-one. And in that instant she knew the time was right and an opportunity would present itself while she was in New Jersey, at Christmas.

It was the Sunday before Christmas. Anita and Jim had gone to Mass with Katy, Anthony and their children. Most of Anthony's family lived in the area and went to the same church. While it took up several pews, they all sat together.

After Mass, a young woman stopped Anthony's brother, Luke. "Hey, Mr. Soldani, it's nice to see you."

"Paige, it's good to see you too." He opened his arms and gave her a hug. "How are things?"

"Okay. You know, I miss Maggie." Tears welled in her eyes. "But deep down, I know she's in a good place. It's just hard right now. It's easier at college. It's pretty lonely here."

Anita could scarcely believe her ears.

"I'm sure it is. Listen, we're celebrating Angie's birthday this evening at Mom and Dad's."

Paige smiled. "Angie was my first-communion partner."

"Your what?"

"My first-communion partner. You know, they matched up an eighth grader in their confirmation year with a kid who was going to make their first-communion? And we did religion stuff together?"

"Hey, that's right. I forgot they did that. I think one of the Danvers boys was mine. Anyway, why don't you come by for dinner?"

"Thanks but I probably shouldn't. I don't know what Dad is doing."

"Nonsense. Bring him too. It's a tough time. I'll tell Mom you're coming."

Anita smiled. As Gertrude had said just before Anita had left the thirteenth century, the universe was unfolding as it should.

After a dinner of the best lasagna Anita had ever eaten she said, "Natalie, dinner was fantastic as always. And *as always*, I overate. You don't mind if I take a little walk for my digestion, do you?"

"Not at all."

Before anyone could offer to go with her, Anita turned to Paige. "You're from this neighborhood, aren't you Paige? Do you want to come with me to make sure I don't get lost?"

"Sure, Mrs. Lewis. I overate too. It's hard not to when it's this delicious. I've been living on college food for the last few months."

They hadn't walked very far when Anita said, "Paige, I think you and I have a mutual acquaintance."

"Do we? I don't think I know anyone in Florida."

"She's not from Florida. At least I don't think she is. Her name is Gertrude."

Paige stopped and stared at Anita. "Gertrude? Pocket watch Gertrude?"

"One and the same."

"How do you know her?"

"She gave me the pocket watch a few years ago. Six to be precise."

"You used it and came back?"

"I did."

"I guess you know she gave it to my sister."

Anita nodded.

Paige shook her head. "Maggie refused to believe it would work. Somehow, I knew…I just knew, it would work." Paige looked down. "I told her if she fell in love she should stay and she did. God, I miss her, but after Maggie died, Gertrude told me she had fallen in love and was very happy."

"Well, my sweet girl, she is very happy indeed."

"You met her?" Paige's tone was incredulous. "When you went back?" Before Anita could respond, Paige's face fell. "But you couldn't have. She only left in June. You said you used the watch six years ago."

"That isn't the way time travel works, and I did meet her. I spent one of the most amazing Christmases of my life with her six years ago in the year twelve-eighty-one."

Joy lit Paige's face. "You did? And she had a good life?"

"To use her words, she is 'blissfully happy'. She wanted me to find you and tell you about her life and her family. When I got back, I wrote everything down, every detail, so you could have it." Anita pulled a copy of her memoir from inside her coat. "This is it. It's my Christmas present to you."

Paige took it in her hands and looked at it as if it were a priceless piece of art. "This is amazing and unbelievable. Thank you. Thank you so much." Paige's brows drew together. "But why did you wait so long? You could have…you could have…"

"No, I couldn't have and all the reasons why are in there. My cell phone number and email address are too. It's probably best if you read it first, but then I will talk to you as often and as long as you wish."

"Thank you, Mrs. Lewis. I don't know what to say." Tears started streaming down her cheeks.

Anita pulled her into a hug. She felt love coursing through her. Maggie's love, Agnes's love and her own love for Maggie, Agnes, and now Paige. She also knew, without a shadow of a doubt, that she had one last mission related to the pocket watch and this one would last as long as she lived. Maggie had sent her to Paige, not just for this moment, but to be a loving presence forever. "You needn't say anything, dear. Merry Christmas."

Paige hugged her back. "Merry Christmas."

About the Author

Ceci started her career as an oncology nurse at a leading research hospital, and eventually became a successful medical writer. In 1991 she married a young Irish carpenter who she met when his brother married her dear friend. They raised their family in central New Jersey but now live with their dogs and birds in paradise, also known as southwest Florida. She recently retired from the pharmaceutical industry and finally is able to devote much of her time to writing "happily ever afters."

The Pocket Watch Chronicles, while related, are all stand-alone books. The Pocket Watch and The Midwife are available as e-books, paperbacks and audiobooks. Once Found is available as and e-book and will be out in paperback soon. The audio version of Once Found is available for free here, on Duncurra's YouTube channel.

Don't miss the Duncurra YouTube channel - https://www.youtube.com/duncurra! You'll find videos of Scotland, Scottish words of the day explained, free audiobooks and much more

More of the Pocket Watch Chronicles

If you enjoyed *The Christmas Present* and haven't read any of the other Pocket Watch Chronicles, you will find Maggie's story in The Pocket Watch.

The Pocket Watch: The Pocket Watch Chronicles

When Maggie Mitchell, is transported to the thirteenth century Highlands will Laird Logan Carr help mend her broken heart or put it in more danger than before?

Generous, kind, and loving, Maggie nearly always puts the needs of others first. So when a mysterious elderly woman gives her an extraordinary pocket watch, telling her it's a conduit to the past, Maggie agrees to give the watch a try, if only to disprove the woman's delusion.

But it works.

Maggie finds herself in the thirteenth century Scottish Highlands, with a handsome warrior who clearly despises her. Her tender soul is caught between her own desire and the disaster she could cause for others. Will she find a way to resolve the trouble and return home within the allotted sixty days? Or will someone worthy earn her heart forever?

The Pocket Watch is available as an <u>e-book</u>, <u>audiobook</u> and <u>paperback</u>

Or get a bigger glimpse of the Soldanis in:

Once Found: The Pocket Watch Chronicles

Elsie thought she had found love.
The handsome young minstrel awoke her desire and his music fed her soul. But just as love was blossoming, the inconceivable happened—Elsie awoke more than seven hundred years in the future, in the body of Dr. Elizabeth Quinn.

Gabriel Soldani thought he had found love several times, only to have it slip from his grasp. In medical school he had fallen hard for Elizabeth Quinn but their careers led them in different directions. When their paths cross again, he hopes they've been given another chance.
There's only one problem…the woman he's never forgotten doesn't remember him.

Once love is found…and then lost…can it be found again?

Once Found is available as an <u>e-book</u>. The audiobook is available for free on the Duncurra YouTube channel.

Meet Dr. Elizabeth Quinn, in:
The Midwife: The Pocket Watch Chronicles

Can a twenty-first century independent woman find her true destiny, in thirteenth century Scotland?

At his father's bidding, Cade MacKenzie begs a favor from Laird Macrae—Lady MacKenzie desperately needs the renowned Macrae midwife. Laird Macrae has no intention of sending his clan's best, instead he passes off Elsie, a young woman with little experience, as the midwife they seek.

But fate—in the form of a mysterious older woman and an extraordinary pocket watch—steps in.

Elizabeth Quinn, a disillusioned obstetrician, is transported to the thirteenth century. She switched souls with Elsie as the old woman said she would but other things don't go quite as expected. Perhaps most unexpected was falling in love.

The Midwife is available as an e-book, audiobook and paperback.

The Choice

Sixty days in another life, another time…it's tempting. Now the decision to accept the pocket watch is yours. What choice will you make?

Sara Wells is in Venice, preparing to leave on a fourteen day cruise to Greece, when Gertrude offers her the pocket watch.

Will she take it? You choose.

If you accept the watch, Sara will travel to eighteenth century Venice where she meets a young Scottish expatriate who owns a small ship building company. Will their love for each other be enough to overcome all obstacles?

If you refuse the watch, Sara will remain in the twenty-first century, where she will encounter a traveler from the past and more intrigue than she can pack into the books she writes.

One choice, two souls, two different happy endings.

The Choice includes two complete, full-length novels

Other Books by Ceci Giltenan

The Fated Hearts Series

Highland Revenge

Does he hate her clan enough to visit his vengeance on her? Or will he listen to her secret and his own heart's yearning?

Hatred lives and breathes between medieval clans who often don't remember why feuds began in the shadowed past.

But Eoin MacKay remembers.

He will never forget how he was treated by Bhaltair MacNicol—the acting head of Clan MacNicol. He was lucky to escape alive, and vows to have revenge.

Years later, as laird of Clan MacKay, he gets his chance when he captures Lady Fiona MacNicol. His desire for revenge is strong but he is beguiled by his captive.

Can he forget his stubborn hatred long enough to listen to the secret she has kept for so long? And once he knows the truth, can he show her she is not alone and forsaken? In the end, is he strong enough to fight the combined hostilities and age-old grudges that demand he give her up?

Highland Revenge is available as an e-book, audio book and paperback.

Highland Echoes

Love echoes.

Grace Breive is strong and independent because she has to be. She has a wee daughter to care for and, having lost her parents and husband, has no one else on whom she can rely. Driven from the only home she has ever known, she travels to Castle Sutherland to find a grandmother she never knew she had.

As Laird Sutherland's heir, Bram Sutherland understands his obligation to enter into a political marriage for the good of the clan, but he is captivated by the beautiful and resilient young mother.

Will Bram and Grace follow the dictates of their hearts, or will echoes from the past force them apart?

Highland Echoes is available as an <u>e-book</u>, <u>audio book</u> and <u>paperback.</u>

Highland Angels

Anna MacKay fears the MacLeods. Andrew MacLeod fears love.

Anna, angry with her brother, took a walk to cool her temper. She had no intention of venturing so close to MacLeod territory—until she saw a wee lad fall through the ice.

Andrew becomes enraged when it appears the MacKay lass has abducted his son, his last precious connection to the wife he lost—until he learns the truth. Anna, risked her life to save his beloved child.

Now there is a chance to end the generations old hate and fear between their clans.

Fate connects them. The desire for peace binds them. Will a rival tear them apart?

Highland Angels is available as an <u>e-book,</u> <u>audio book</u> and <u>paperback</u>.

The Duncurra Series

Highland Solution

The first book in the Duncurra Series, available as <u>e-book</u>, <u>audiobook</u> and <u>paperback</u>. An <u>Inspirational Version</u> is also available which has been edited to remove explicit intimate scenes.

Laird Niall MacIan needs Lady Katherine Ruthven's dowry to relieve his clan's crushing debt but he has no intention of giving her his heart in the bargain.

Niall MacIan, a Highland laird, desperately needs funds to save his impoverished clan. Lady Katherine Ruthven, a lowland heiress, is rumored to be "unmarriageable" and her uncle hopes to be granted her title and lands when the king sends her to a convent.

King David II anxious to strengthen his alliances sees a solution that will give Ruthven the title he wants, and MacIan the money he needs. Laird MacIan will receive Lady Katherine's hand along with her substantial dowry and her uncle will receive her lands and title.

Lady Katherine must forfeit everything in exchange for a husband who does not want to be married and believes all women to be self-centered and deceitful. Can the lovely and gentle Katherine mend his heart and build a life with him or will he allow the treachery of others to destroy them?

Highland Courage

The second book in the Duncurra Series, available as e-book, audiobook and paperback. An Inspirational Version is also available which has been edited to remove explicit intimate scenes.

Her parents want a betrothal, but Mairead MacKenzie can't get married without revealing her secret and no man will wed her once he knows.

Plain in comparison to her siblings and extremely reserved, Mairead has been called "MacKenzie's Mouse" since she was a child. No one knows the reason for her timidity and she would just as soon keep it that way. When her parents arrange a betrothal to Laird Tadhg Matheson she is horrified. She only sees one way to prevent an old secret from becoming a new scandal.

Tadhg Matheson admires and respects the MacKenzies. While an alliance with them through marriage to Mairead would be in his clan's best interest, he knows Laird MacKenzie seeks a closer alliance with another clan. When Tadhg learns of her terrible shyness and her youngest brother's fears about her, Tadhg offers for her anyway.

Secrets always have a way of revealing themselves. With Tadhg's unconditional love, can Mairead find the strength and courage she needs to handle the consequences when they do?

Highland Intrigue

The third book in the Duncurra Series, available as <u>e-book</u>, <u>audiobook</u> and <u>paperback</u>. An <u>Inspirational Version</u> is also available which has been edited to remove explicit intimate scenes.

Lady Gillian MacLennan's clan needs a leader, but the last person on earth she wants as their laird is Fingal MacIan. She can neither forgive nor forget that his mother killed her father, and, by doing so, created Clan MacLennan's current desperate circumstances.

King David knows a weak clan, without a laird, can change quickly from a simple annoyance to a dangerous liability, and he cannot ignore the turmoil. The MacIan's owe him a great debt, so when he makes Fingal MacIan laird of clan MacLennan and requires that he marry Lady Gillian, Fingal is in no position to refuse.

In spite of the challenge, Fingal is confident he can rebuild her clan, ease her heartache and win her affection. However, just as love awakens, the power struggle takes a deadly turn. Can he protect her from the unknown long enough to uncover the plot against them? Or will all be lost, destroying the happiness they seek in each other's arms?

About Duncurra

Duncurra is a small independent publishing company. We highly value the heart and soul, energy, time, and talent that our authors pour into their stories. Unlike many independent publishers, we help authors build their readership by investing significantly in marketing platforms to complement the author's own promotional efforts.

We are particularly proud of our YouTube presence and ever increasing subscribership there, which is unique to the publishing industry.

Whether you are a reader, an established author, or an aspiring author, we have a lot to offer. We take the reader experience to a new level, connecting authors and readers in unprecedented ways.

Visit our website at www.duncurra.com.

To stay up to date on all Duncurra releases, sales, giveaways and more, sign up for our newsletter here: https://tinyletter.com/duncurra

Experience the difference.
Experience Duncurra!

Other titles published by Duncurra LLC

Award Winning, New York Times Bestselling Author
Kathryn Lynn Davis
<u>Highland Awakening</u>
<u>Sing to Me of Dreams</u>

Award Winning, Bestselling Author
Lily Baldwin

Highland Outlaw Series
(All of the Highland Outlaw series are complete standalone stories and can be read in any order.)

Jack: A Scottish Outlaw

Quinn: A Scottish Outlaw

Rory: A Scottish Outlaw

Alec: A Scottish Outlaw

Coming Fall 2017: Rose: A Scottish Outlaw

Ford Murphy

Taking the Town

Stephanie Joyce Cole

Compass North

MJ Platt

Somewhere Montana

B.J. Scott

Talisman of Light

Forever and Beyond

Jennifer Siddoway

Dealing with the Devil

The Devil's Due

Coming Fall 2017, the final installment of the Earthwalker Trilogy: Down in Flames

Made in the USA
Columbia, SC
03 July 2019